UNDERCOVER KILLERS

Fargo made for the cabin. To his rear, a piercing shriek rang out. Whirling, he saw the bushes shaking and rustling fifty feet away, and thought he saw Floyd clinging to one as if for dear life.

"Help me, mister! God in heaven, help me!"

It was no act. The fear in Havershaw's voice was genuine. Drawing the Colt, Fargo raced to lend his aid as the vegetation erupted in a riot of snapping brush and desperate screams.

"They've got me! Help! Help!"

Fargo was halfway there when the sounds abruptly ceased and the undergrowth stopped moving. Rounding the last thicket, he stopped in consternation. A severely trampled patch of weeds marked the spot where Havershaw had been, and near it lay a freshly broken tree limb Floyd must have torn off in his struggles. But the man was nowhere to be seen.

It was as if the earth had yawned wide and swallowed Havershaw whole. . . .

THE

TRAILSMAN

#251

UTAH UPROAR

by

Jon Sharpe

A SIGNET BOOK

SIGNET
Published by New American Library, a division of
Penguin Putnam Inc., 375 Hudson Street,
New York, New York 10014, U.S.A.
Penguin Books Ltd, 80 Strand,
London WC2R 0RL, England
Penguin Books Australia Ltd, Ringwood,
Victoria, Australia
Penguin Books Canada Ltd, 10 Alcorn Avenue,
Toronto, Ontario, Canada M4V 3B2
Penguin Books (N.Z.) Ltd, 182–190 Wairau Road,
Auckland 10, New Zealand

Penguin Books Ltd, Registered Offices:
Harmondsworth, Middlesex, England

First published by Signet, an imprint of New American Library,
a division of Penguin Putnam Inc.

First Printing, September 2002
10 9 8 7 6 5 4 3 2 1

The first chapter of this title originally appeared in *Arizona Ambush,*
the two hundred fiftieth volume in this series.

REGISTERED TRADEMARK—MARCA REGISTRADA

Printed in the United States of America

PUBLISHER'S NOTE
This is a work of fiction. Names, characters, places, and incidents either are
the product of the author's imagination or are used fictitiously, and any
resemblance to actual persons, living or dead, events, or locales is entirely
coincidental.

The Trailsman

Beginnings . . . they bend the tree and they mark the man. Skye Fargo was born when he was eighteen. Terror was his midwife, vengeance his first cry. Killing spawned Skye Fargo, ruthless, cold-blooded murder. Out of the acrid smoke of gunpowder still hanging in the air, he rose, cried out a promise never forgotten.

The Trailsman they began to call him all across the West: searcher, scout, hunter, the man who could see where others only looked, his skills for hire but not his soul, the man who lived each day to the fullest, yet trailed each tomorrow. Skye Fargo, the Trailsman, the seeker who could take the wildness of a land and the wanting of a woman and make them his own.

*The Great Salt Lake Desert, 1861—
unexplored, unrelenting, and certain
death for the unwary.*

1

The tall man in buckskins was about seventy-five miles west of Salt Lake City when a whirlwind of death roared down on him.

Skye Fargo had left Salt Lake several days before, bound for California. It was the middle of the summer and daytime temperatures were well over one hundred degrees. As a result, he traveled at night rather than during the day in order to spare his pinto stallion from being roasted alive. Now, well out into the Great Salt Lake Desert, Fargo felt a sudden gust of wind on his bearded face. His piercing lake-blue eyes scanned the star-sprinkled heavens to the west, seeking sign of an approaching storm. But the sky was crystal clear, the night serene. Not even a single star was blotted out by clouds.

Fargo had been following a rutted track that wound across the desert. In a couple more days he would reach the small settlement of Wendover. Until then, he had to be on his guard against roving bands of hostile Utes. The tribe was at odds with the Mormons over the loss of land. Not all that long ago a bitter war had been fought, and while a truce was supposedly in effect, a number of whites had disappeared without a trace.

Fargo also had to be on his watch against the elements. Thunderstorms were common this time of year. For a rider to be caught in the open in one was as dangerous as being caught by a Ute war party; flash floods and lightning had claimed many a life. So when another gust of wind buffeted him, Fargo became concerned. It was much too strong for a typical breeze. He sniffed the air but detected no trace of moisture, as there would be if a storm front were approaching.

That left one possibility.

Every nerve taut, Fargo rode on. He hoped he was wrong. He hoped there wouldn't be any more gusts of wind. But he hadn't gone another fifty yards when the strongest one yet buffeted him, nearly taking his hat off.

"I don't like this fella," Fargo said aloud to the Ovaro as he jammed his hat back down onto his head. He had a habit of talking to the pinto during long, lonely stretches on the trail. The stallion snorted, as if in agreement, and pricked up its ears as if it had caught a faint sound.

Fargo listened but heard nothing. He sniffed the night air again but smelled nothing. He tried to convince himself he was making too much out of it. That all would be well. That the stallion must have heard a coyote or a mountain lion.

Then the wind returned with a vengeance, a ferocious blast that nearly took Fargo's breath away and whipped the fringe on his buckskins. A few stinging grains of sand pelted him, harbingers of much worse to come.

"Sandstorm!" Fargo breathed. They had to find a spot to take shelter. He surveyed the flat, bleak landscape but all he saw were a few scattered boulders. To the north and west lay more of the same. To the south, though, was an isolated mountain range rarely visited by either whites or red man. There were plenty of places to wait out Nature's temper tantrum in relative safety. A prick of his spurs galvanized the pinto into a trot, but he doubted the windstorm would hold off long enough for them to get there. Unfortunately, he was right.

Fargo had barely gone a mile when the wind doubled in intensity. Fine particles of sand pelted every exposed inch of his skin. He had to squint to keep it from getting into his eyes. In the distance wind-spawned shrieks keened like a chorus of the damned unleashed from the pit of hell.

The Ovaro gamely trotted on, seemingly impervious

to the barrage of sand. But Fargo knew better. Drawing rein, he dismounted, hastily opened a saddlebag, and took out his spare shirt. He stepped in front of the stallion and raised it to tie it over the Ovaro's eyes to shield them. But just as he did, and especially powerful blast of screaming wind tore it from his grasp and flung the flapping garment against the Ovaro. The horse did what most any other would do; whinnying in fright, it shied and pranced wildly away.

"No!" Fargo hollered. He lunged to grab hold of the reins but his fingers closed on thin air.

The Ovaro was in full flight, the shirt still partially wrapped around its head and upper neck, the shirt sleeves flapping wildly.

Fargo ran after it. A useless gesture, since within moments his horse had melted into the murk. He drew up short, staggered by the cruel trick fate had played. To be stranded afoot was bad enough. To be stranded with a sandstorm about to break in all its raging elemental might was a calamity. Not only for him, but also for the stallion. Left on its own, exposed and unprotected, the Ovaro might very well die.

Nearby was a waist-high boulder. Nor much cover, but enough that if Fargo were to curl up into a ball at its base and covered his head with both arms, he could wait out the worst of the ordeal to come. But if he did, he gave up any hope of recovering the Ovaro. He doggedly ran on.

The wind pummeled him with invisible fists. The sand stung like a swarm of angry bees. And all the while the shrieking grew louder. It wouldn't be long now. The sandstorm was almost on top of him. Fargo's boots sent up fine plumes of the whitish sand with every stride, plumes instantly blown apart like so many wisps of smoke.

Unbidden, Fargo remembered the time he came on a pair of skeletons in an Arizona desert. A prospector and a mule had been caught in a sandstorm and sought haven on the lee side of a dune. They ended up buried alive. If a freak rainstorm hadn't later washed away part of the dune shortly before he happened by, no one would ever have known.

Then there was the Brockman party, a wagon train bound for the promised land of Oregon. Eleven families had been caught far from anywhere when a sandstorm descended upon them. An army patrol found the survivors. All four of them. Their wagons were in ruins, most upended, the canvas tops ripped to ribbons. And every last animal had either run off, never to be seen again, or perished outright.

Fargo gave a toss of his head, derailing his train of thought. There were also people who had lived through sandstorms and he intended to be one of them. But first he had to find the Ovaro. He kept hoping the pinto hadn't run that far. At any moment he might stumble across it.

Visibility had been reduced to twenty feet and was lessening rapidly. One arm in front of his eyes, Fargo shouted, "Here, boy! Over here, big fella!" But his cry was smothered by the wind.

How far Fargo ran, he couldn't say. Maybe a mile. Maybe two. Suddenly the sky was rent by a titanic howl of unearthly proportions and the sandstorm swooped down in all its terrible might, engulfing the desert in a cyclonic gale that had to be experienced to be believed.

In the blink of an eye, Fargo couldn't see any further than the end of his arm. So much sand was in the air, it hurt to breathe. It got into his nose and filled his mouth. His eyes were mercilessly battered and wouldn't stop watering. Pressing both forearms over his face, he stumbled on, half-blinded, barely able to catch a decent breath. He needed to stop and dig in. *But where?* He cast about for a boulder, a gully, any place that would afford some small measure of protection. But there was none.

To complicate matters, Fargo had lost all sense of direction. Without the stars to guide him, he wasn't sure if he was still heading south. He might be traveling east or west. Slowing, he peered hard into the swirling tempest, desperate to find cover. But his eyes were so irritated by sand, the world around him was a watery blur.

"Damn!" Fargo swore aloud, and promptly regretted it when a fistful of sand was blown halfway down his throat. He tried to spit it out, but in opening his mouth he admitted more. Gagging, he doubled over. He spit out as much of the sand as he could, but his mouth and throat were still layered with it.

Without warning, a wall of wind slammed into him, nearly bowling Fargo over. It started to tear his hat off. He clutched at the brim but was too slow. The hat went sailing off into the storm.

Fargo lurched forward, groping blindly. He had to keep his eyes nearly shut. Not that they were of much use anyway. His right book scraped a boulder and he bent low to gauge the size. It didn't come any higher than the middle of his shins and wouldn't afford the haven he needed. Struggling to keep his balance against the pummeling wind, he trudged on.

Although folks said he was as strong as a bull, Fargo had his limits. This relentless onslaught of the wind, this ceaseless bombardment of sand, were more than any man could endure indefinitely. His strength and his energy, were swiftly being sapped. Then his left boot bumped something in his path. His questing fingers found a cluster of large boulders. Carefully easing in among them, Fargo sank to his knees and lowered his forehead to the ground. Sand still pelted him, but nowhere near as much. And here he was spared the brunt of the rampaging wind. Wrapping his arms around his head, he resigned himself to being stuck there for a spell.

Fargo couldn't stop thinking about the Ovaro. He had ridden that horse from one end of the country to the other, from the Gulf of Mexico to the Canadian border, from the Mississippi River to the Pacific Ocean. Seldom had it ever let him down. He would sooner part with an arm or a leg, and the thought of the Ovaro out there somewhere, helpless and alone, had him grinding his teeth in frustration.

Around him chaos reigned. Caterwauling like a million wildcats, the wind never slackened. Nor did the blistering onslaught of sand. Fargo could fee it crawl up under his shirt and down into his pants. Without a blanket to cover himself with, he was forced to endure whatever the storm dished out.

Fargo's eyes were on fire, but he resisted an urge to wipe his sleeve against them. It would only aggravate them further. He needed water to do the job properly. Unfortunately, his canteen was on the Ovaro. So were his rifle, his bedroll, and practically every personal article he owned. He chose not to dwell on the consequences should he fail to reclaim them.

The minutes dragged into an eternity. It might have been two hours later, it might have been four, when Fargo realized the banshee wail was tapering off and the tornadic upheaval was dying. He raised his head, wincing at a cramp in his neck, and was startled to discover the gap between the boulders had filled up with sand past his hips. He could barely move his legs. With an effort, he rose onto his knees. The night was an impenetrable curtain of darkness, the sky was obscured. He wouldn't be able to get his bearings until he could see the stars again.

The wind was down to a whisper. Relieved the storm hadn't lasted any longer, Fargo placed his hands flat against a boulder to rise, then paused. From the west wafted a shrill whine. It might be nothing. Then again, it could be that the storm wasn't over, that this was a lull before another blast was unleashed. He listened intently, and sure enough, the whine slowly grew until it resembled the cry of a woman in dire distress.

Fargo bent low just as the sandstorm renewed its assault with magnified ferocity. What had gone before was mild compared to the volcanic eruption that now took place. Within moments Fargo was being scoured by buckets of sand hurled by a whirlwind of titanic proportions. And all he could do was hunker down and bear it.

The level of the sand encasing Fargo steadily rose. It was soon above his belt. At the rate the gap was filling, it wouldn't be long before he ended up sharing the fate of the man who had been buried alive. He pushed at the growing pile to shove as much as he could from between the boulders, but for every handful he dislodged, the wind deposited a gallon to take its place.

Grains were trickling into Fargo's ears and down into his boots. He spat repeatedly but he couldn't get the hard grains out of his mouth.

It was then, at the height of the sandstorm, that Fargo thought he heard a whinny coming from somewhere nearby. Believing it to be the Ovaro, he automatically sat up again, full into the wind. It violently shoved him against a boulder. Inadvertently, he opened his eyes all the way, and was spiked by tiny daggers that threatened to strip his sight away.

Doubling over, Fargo covered his eyes with his hands. He had no choice but to stay there as long as he could, even at the risk of being buried alive. The Ovaro, he reluctantly conceded, was on its own until it was safe for him to move about.

Inky blackness veiled the world. Fargo peeked between his fingers now and then but saw no sign that the storm was abating. If it didn't stop soon, he would have a decision to make. Should he stay there and be buried or go in search of better sanctuary? It was a case of damned if he did, damned if he didn't. Whichever he chose, the prospects were grim.

Fargo opted to stay put. Out in the open he wouldn't last sixty seconds. His skin would be flayed from his body and his lungs would succumb to the lack of breathable air. A decade down the road someone might stumble across his remains and have the decency to bury them. If not, his bleached skull would serve as a warning to all those who came after.

Fargo went to shift his right arm to relieve a pain in his elbow, and couldn't. The sand had risen to within a hand's width of his shoulders, pinning his arms in place. In a fit of anger he pulled loose, and in so doing more sand got into his nose and mouth. It felt as if he were inhaling shards of glass.

Of the many ways Fargo had imagined dying, this wasn't one of them. Frontiersmen lived notoriously short lives. Each and every day they had to contend with a thousand and one ways of dying. Wild beasts, painted hostiles, Nature's temper tantrums, all of which took a constant toll. Fargo always thought he would die in a gunfight or in a battle with warriors out to lift his scalp, not smothered to death in a sandstorm.

The level continued to rise. It was now just below his chin. Fargo had to get out of there before it was too late. Surging upward, he rose a few inches but couldn't fully straighten. The sand hemmed him like a straitjacket. By twisting back and forth he began to loosen its grip, but in the meantime the storm pounded him without quarter. His face hurt abominably. He dared not do more than crack his eyelids, for to open them wider invited permanent blindness.

With a tremendous wrench, Fargo tore clear and tottered out from among the boulders. He had gone from the proverbial frying pan into the proverbial fire. Out in the open, the full weight of the storm bore down his shoulders. The hammering wind drove him to this knees, the rampant sand cut and stung like a thousand tiny knives.

Willing his legs to work, Fargo staggered forward in search of shelter. He had no idea in which direction he was going. Again and again, he bumped into small boulders, spiking pain up his legs. Several times he tripped, and once he fell to his hands and knees. Deprived of his senses, he was as helpless as an infant. A reminder, as if any were needed, that in the scheme of things man was no more than a flickering flame on a candle, to be extinguished at Nature's whim.

On and on Fargo plodded, but sanctuary was denied him. Gradually his energy was sapped as his great strength ebbed. His legs became wooden, his arms stiff. Each time he swallowed, he swore his throat was being ripped raw. It was like swallowing a cup of tiny thorns.

Just when it seemed the most hopeless, Fargo was dealt the cruelest card yet. His next step was into empty space. Instinctively, he jerked back, but his legs were swept out from under him and he tumbled end over end.

A jarring blow brought his careening plunge to a halt. The darkness deepened and his mind swam in pitch.

Rolling onto his stomach, Fargo got his hands under his chest. He levered upward, only to have his sinews betray him. His cheek smacked the earth. He wanted to rise but couldn't. His last sensation was of the remorseless sand pelting him. His last thought was that this was a damned stupid way to die.

Pain restored Fargo to the land of the living. He was afloat in a relentless sea of agony. When he opened his eyes, it was like having them spiked by a Comanche lance. A low cry escaped his lips, and for several seconds he thought he would pass out again.

Asserting his iron self-control, Fargo attempted to stand up but couldn't. Something was pressing down on his back and legs. One glance explained his plight. He was on his stomach at the bottom of a dry wash, buried in sand almost to his neck. His lips felt dry and cracked, his throat was parched. Moistening his tongue, he swallowed, provoking more torment.

Fargo's left arm wouldn't budge but his right would. Exercising care not to get more sand into his eyes, Fargo pumped his right arm up and down and back and forth until it slid out, then scooped off enough stand for him to sit up. The position of the sun told him it was the middle of the morning. Rising on unsteady legs, he climbed toward the rim.

Fargo's skin was raw to the touch. His cheeks were puffy, his eyelids swollen. He could see, but every time he blinked, it felt like he was rubbing a cactus across his pupils. Without thinking, he ran a hand through his tangled hair and sand rained down. It was caked to his clothes, layered thick under them, and filled his boots to their brims.

The landscape that met his questing gaze was barren and lifeless. Only sand, sand everywhere, dotted by occasional islands of rock. To the south, not all that far away, reared towering stone ramparts. It was the mountain range that didn't have a name, a range as remote from civilization as the moon is from the earth. Apparently, he had walked a lot farther than he thought.

Which way should he go? That was the crucial question. Fargo gazed northward, where, miles off, the trail to Oregon lay. He might be able to reach it. If so, some other travelers might come along and help him. The mountains were a lot closer, though. And there was a chance, however slim, that in them he would find the one thing he needed most: water. There might be a spring or a hidden tank. Without it, he wouldn't last more than a few days, if that. Already the temperature had to be above ninety, and would soon eclipse the century mark.

Fargo considered holing up until nightfall, but he was so battered and sore and worn out that the rest wouldn't do him much good. Besides, there wasn't much shade to be had anywhere in his vicinity. He started out but had only gone a few steps when the feel of sand between his toes reminded him there was something he must do.

Grunting from the pain, Fargo slowly peeled off his buckskin shirt and shook it out. He removed his bandanna, boots, ankle knife, socks, and pants and gave them the same treatment. His holster was crammed with sand, so he upended it. A check of his Colt revealed there was some in the barrel and the cylinder. Removing the cartridges, he blew into the barrel and then wiped the revolver on the inside of his shirt. As best he could tell, he got most of the sand out, but the Colt would need a thorough cleaning at the earliest opportunity. Fargo's hair was matted with the stuff. He ran his fingers through it at least a dozen times, but it would take a bath to clean him proper.

The whole while, the sun beat down on his bare skin. Fargo hurriedly dressed, tied the bandanna around his forehead to absorb sweat, and headed out once again. A lot of the stiffness in his legs soon vanished, but his face was a constant mask of pain. He needed water, needed it badly.

Wildlife needed it, too. If Fargo could find a game trail, it might lead him to some. But although he diligently scoured the desert, he saw no evidence of life other than his own. The sandstorm had seen to that. It had obliterated whatever sign there might have been.

Fargo perspired profusely. His buckskins became soaked, and for a while the damp feeling brought a margin of relief. The mountains loomed closer, awesome monoliths of solid stone sculpted by a gigantic chisel. And not a tree anywhere to be seen. Not so much as a single bush.

The burning sun was almost directly overheard when a shadow flitted across the ground at Fargo's feet. Squinting up, he discovered he had aerial company. Four buzzards were circling him. "Not yet, you mangy bastards," he declared defiantly. Brave talk, but his body was in a lot worse shape than he was willing to admit. His eyes were now swollen half-shut, and his lips were as thick as his thumbs. He was sure he must look like something out of a child's worst nightmare.

By early afternoon Fargo's entire body was throbbing. His temples pounded to the beat of his heart and he had difficulty forming coherent thoughts. His tongue was twice its normal size and his throat was as dry as the surrounding waste of sun-baked sand.

By late afternoon, Fargo was unsure whether he could make it. The mountains were farther than they appeared. Another five miles, if he wasn't mistaken. Five miles of being roasted alive. Five miles of sheer torture. His feet felt fit to burst his boots at the seams but he forced them to plod on. Soon his mind shut down and he moved mechanically, more out of impulse than design. Now and again his eyelids drooped shut, but he didn't stop. He couldn't. His very life was at stake.

So sensitive had Fargo's body become to the stifling inferno that when there was a subtle change, he opened his eyes to find himself standing in the shadow of a jagged peak. He had reached the mountains! Eagerly, he lurched toward a low stone slope. Scaling it took every ounce of energy he could muster. From the top spread a vista of rolling hills broken by intermittent rocky heights. And not a trace of green anywhere.

A groan escaped him. Fargo tried to lick his severely dry lips but had no saliva to apply to them. He shambled to the next hill, and from there to the next, and so it went for the next hour and a half. The sun wouldn't set until eight, so he had plenty of daylight left. Too much, for night would bring welcome coolness and vastly needed relief.

By six or so, Fargo was virtually on his last legs. Only his superb stamina kept him in motion and it wouldn't suffice indefinitely. Soon he would reach the point of total collapse, and that would be that. Come morning, the buzzards would close in for their meal. If he were too weak to lift a finger, they would devour him alive, ripping his flesh from his bones with their powerful beaks, then gulping the morsels whole. They would commence with his eyes and nose and other soft parts, and go from there. It would be a gruesome end, one he wouldn't wish on his worst enemy.

Belatedly, Fargo's brain registered his boots were no longer scraping stone. The ground under him felt softer. Looking down, he beheld dirt. Wonderful, life-supporting dirt. The terrain was changing. Another ten yards and he saw a dry bush. Then a whole acre of scrub. And beyond, perhaps a hundred yards, stood the most glorious sight in all creation: a tree.

Newfound energy coursed through Fargo's veins. Where there was vegetation, there had to be water! He broke into an awkward jog, lumbering along like an animated corpse. Suddenly he gasped and stopped dead. Clearly imprinted in the soft soil were hoofprints, *tracks made by a shod horse*. It had to be the Ovaro. Somehow the stallion had survived the storm and was no doubt desperately seeking water, the same as he was. Only where he had to rely on his sand-blasted eyes, the stallion had its excellent sense of smell to guide it. Horses could smell water from a mile off. All he had to do was follow the Ovaro and it would lead him right where he needed to go.

His cracked lips splitting in a lopsided grin, Fargo threaded through the brush to the solitary tree. A juniper, if he wasn't mistaken. Shielding his eyes with his palm, he spied more not fifty yards to the southwest. The Ovaro's tracks led straight toward them.

Fargo ran, or engaged in an act that most closely resembled it. He was thinking of all the cool, sweet water he would drink, and how nice it would be to plunge his face in and keep it there for as long as he could hold his breath.

A whinny broke the stillness, punctuated moments later by the feral snarls of predators.

Fear gripped Fargo. His hand dropped to the smooth butt of his Colt as he charged in among the trees along a clearly defined game path overlaid by the stallion's hoofprints. And overlaying *these* were fresh pad marks. He heard another whinny and a series of growls, and then he was through the trees and standing on the lip of a shallow basin. On the opposite side, at the base of a low cliff, glistened a shimmering spring. Beside it, backed against the cliff, was the Ovaro.

Five snarling coyotes had cornered the stallion. Ordinarily, coyotes posed little threat to a full-grown horse. But these were half-starved. Spread out in a half-circle, they were slinking toward their prey with their fangs bared.

Fargo drew his Colt. He would drop one or two and the rest would scatter. Thumbing back the hammer, he took deliberate aim at the nearest and squeezed the trigger. But no shot rang out. There was a raspy metallic *click,* and that was it. The gun had misfired. It was all the sand in the barrel, Fargo realized, and he swore.

The nearest coyote and another heard him. Spinning around, they let out with savage yips and advanced.

2

Coyotes rarely attacked humans. A bold one might snatch an untended baby or pounce on a small child, but nine times out of ten they fled from adults. Not this time. As three of the gaunt beasts slunk toward the Ovaro, two crept toward Skye Fargo, their heads low to the ground, their teeth glistening viciously in the sunlight.

Fargo thumbed back the Colt's hammer a second time and once again stroked the trigger. Again the revolver misfired. Without it, in his weakened state he would be easy to bring down. But not without a fight. He still had his Arkansas toothpick, nestled in its ankle sheath. Abruptly sinking onto one knee, he slid his free hand up under his pant leg and gripped the knife's hilt.

At that exact same instant, the foremost coyote growled and rushed him. Jaws gaping wide to rip and rend, it launched itself into the air.

Fargo heaved upright, swinging the toothpick in a glittering arc that met the coyote in midair. Razor-sharp steel sliced deep into fur and sinew. Simultaneously, Fargo sidestepped, and the coyote went plunging past him, a scarlet geyser spurting from its severed jugular. Fargo pivoted toward the second coyote, but it had already sprung, and as he rotated, it slammed into his chest, bowling him over. He wound up flat on his back with the coyote on top of him, trying to fasten its slavering jaws onto his neck.

Fargo pistol-whipped the animal across the head. Were he his usual self, the blow would have rendered the coyote unconscious. But his depleted strength was barely enough to rock the coyote onto its hindquarters. Thrusting with the toothpick, he buried the blade as far as it would go.

An ear-splitting howl was ripped from the coyote's throat. It leaped to one side, or tried to, for the blade had pieced its heart and it was dead before it finished its spring. Landing in a disjointed sprawl, it collapsed and was still.

Fargo pushed himself erect. He had very little energy left and three coyotes remained. They were trying to get at the stallion, but the Ovaro's flailing hooves were keeping them momentarily at bay. As Fargo looked on, one darted in too close and was met full-on by a sweeping hoof that caved in the coyote's skull like a hammer crushing an over-ripe melon. The coyote fell in its tracks, brain matter oozing from the cavity.

"Hang on, boy!" Fargo cried, and moved to help. His legs wouldn't work as fast as he wanted and his breathing was labored but he still had some fight left in him.

Then a searing pang shot up Fargo's left calf, and he was brought to a stop. Shifting, he glanced down. The coyote whose throat he had slit was still alive, and it had imbedded its teeth in his leg.

Fargo stabbed at the beasts's neck, but the coyote nimbly skipped aside and came at him again, down low, going for his ankle. A quick sidestep saved him, but he couldn't avoid the animal indefinitely. Sooner or later his exhaustion would show and the coyote would bring him down.

Fargo couldn't say what made him do what he did next. Perhaps it was reflex. Perhaps it was frustration. For although the Colt had misfired twice, he shoved it at the coyote and squeezed off another shot. It was hard to say which of them was more surprised by the resultant blast, but it was safe to say the coyote's surprise was more fleeting. The slug caught it flush between the eyes.

Pivoting, Fargo fired at one of the two remaining beasts. Again the revolver belched lead and smoke. Again a coyote crumpled. The last member of the pack had learned from his companions' fate, and he was off like a fur-covered streak. Within seconds the mountains swallowed him.

Grinning wearily, Fargo tottered on spongy legs toward the Ovaro. "We did it, boy!" He reached out and the Ovaro sniffed his hand, then nuzzled against him.

Fargo went to pat its neck, and paused, appalled. The sandstorm had inflicted a terrible toll. Whole patches of hide had been scraped raw and were bleeding. Its mane and tail were as matted as his hair, if not more so. But most appalling of all were the Ovaro's eyes. They were swollen almost completely shut and pus was oozing from both ends. Its mouth was also puffy, but nowhere near as bad.

"God, no," Fargo breathed as the full significance hit him. The Ovaro could well be blind.

Careful where he touched, Fargo rubbed the pinto's neck and chest. A constriction formed in his throat and he had to cough to relieve it. Then, grasping the reins, he led the Ovaro the few feet to the spring. Judging by how greedily it gulped the water, it had been interrupted by the coyotes before it could slake its thirst.

Replacing the Colt and the toothpick, Fargo eased onto his hands and knees and lowered his entire head in. The sensation was exquisite. Overwhelming relief flooded over him, and for a precious minute he was pain free. Then, raising his head, he took a few light sips. The water was delicious beyond measure. He knew enough not to drink too much, and after a bit he slowly sat up.

The stallion was still guzzling like an alcoholic from a keg. "That's enough for now," Fargo said softly, and pulled the pinto a dozen yards into the shade. He examined his saddle and was pleased to find it intact. The same couldn't be side of his bedroll. It was missing. So was his canteen. His saddlebags had come partly untied, but thankfully he hadn't lost any of his few possessions. Most vital of all, the Henry was still snug in its saddle scabbard although the scabbard contained enough sand to fill a whiskey bottle.

Stripping off the saddle and saddle blanket, Fargo set his effects against the cliff for the time being. He had lost his spare shirt but he still had a spare set of buckskin pants. Removing them, he drew the toothpick and cut a long, wide strip from one of the pant legs. He soaked it in the spring, then gingerly applied the strip to the stallion's ravaged eyes but didn't tie it in order not to aggravate matters.

The Ovaro was as exhausted as Fargo. Hanging its head, it barely moved.

"There's got to be more that I can do," Fargo said aloud. His elation at recovering his mount was tempered by the realization he might yet lose it. Not from the wounds, which were superficial, but from the damage to its eyes. A blind horse would be of no use to him. He would be forced to sell it to someone kindly enough to take care of it the rest of its days. A notion he couldn't countenance. Losing the Ovaro would be like losing a best friend. "There's got to be more," he repeated.

But what, exactly? Fargo had lived among the Sioux. He had spent time with the Shoshones. With the Cheyenne. He was intimately familiar with a dozen other tribes. As a result, his knowledge of their healing arts was second to none. Indians used a wide range of medicinal cures the white man knew nothing about.

Among them were treatments specifically for horses. The advent of the horse had forever changed the Indian way of life, and in warrior societies, prized war horses were held in the highest esteem. Small wonder, then, special steps were taken when one was ill or wounded. Tea was concocted from wild melons and used to cure worms. The leaves of the yarrow plant were boiled and applied to boils. Milkweed juice was effective in relieving a back rubbed sore from too much riding.

Eye treatments for horses were common. The Paiutes relied on the acacia plant to cure inflammation of the eyes. The Blackfeet used the alumroot plant. The Shoshones were partial to blue flax roots. None of which did Fargo any good. He needed a plant that grew in the immediate area. Antelope brush was his best bet. A poultice brewed from its bark was extremely potent in relieving inflammation and reducing pus.

Moving to the basin's rim, Fargo scanned the terrain in all directions. To the south there was a lot more vegetation. More junipers, some grass, the inevitable array of weeds, but not a patch of antelope brush in sight.

Descending, Fargo studied the soft soil rimming the spring. Out of the dim past of his childhood surfaced the recollection of a way of treating bee and wasp stings, and the swelling they caused. Taking a rock with a rough edge, he scooped out enough dirt for his purpose; making mud. Until he could find a suitable plant it was the best he could do.

The Ovaro nickered and tried to pull its head away when Fargo daubed the first handful over its eyes. They were so horribly swollen that he applied the mud as lightly as possible. When he was done, he gently wrapped the buckskin strip over the mud to hold it in place. Then, lying near the spring, he applied some to his own eyes and lay back to rest.

Fargo reckoned on staying there as long as it took for them to mend. The spring provided ample water, there was grass for the pinto, and, with a little luck, by day's end he would have enough meat to last him a good long spell.

The fatigue Fargo had been refusing to acknowledge would no longer be denied. He dozed off and slept soundly for over an hour. The *clop* of one of the Ovaro's hooves woke him. The stallion was pawing the ground. Something must be wrong.

Fargo reached up to remove the mud so he could see and discovered it had practically dried. His eyes were itching fiercely. Quickly wiping them clear, he dipped a hand in the spring and washed off the residue. A check of the basin revealed no cause for alarm. The Ovaro was still stomping, though. He guessed the dry mud was to blame, and he soon had it off. Once he did the stallion quieted.

"I honestly can't say if this will help or not, big fella, but it's better than nothing," Fargo said. He applied a second coat, and from then on, throughout the remainder of the day, he changed the mud about once an hour.

Toward twilight Fargo led the pinto to the center of the basin, ripped a clump of grass out by the roots, and held it under the Ovaro's nose. The stallion's big teeth sheared through it like a saber through butter, and soon it was hungrily filling its belly. Leaving it ground-hitched, Fargo sat down by the rock cliff to do something he should have done a lot earlier.

From his saddlebags Fargo took a folded cloth and a small kit that contained the few tools needed to take apart a firearm. He stripped both the Colt and the Henry and thoroughly cleaned them. He couldn't afford another misfire, not when the cost might be his life.

On the frontier guns were as essential to a man as his heart and lungs. They were regarded as tools, like an axe or a knife, and no frontiersman went anywhere without one. A gun put food on a man's plate, kept his scalp from being raised by hostiles, and took care of cutthroats inclined to do him harm. Fargo had been carrying a pistol since he was in his teens. It was such a natural part of him, that he felt naked walking around unhitched whenever he visited cities and towns where guns were not allowed to be worn in public.

The sand had seeped into the Colt between the hammer and the firing pin, which explained why the revolver had failed to shoot. In the Henry, sand coated the inside of the barrel and had sifted into the breach. By the time he was done, they were as sand-free and shiny as the day they were first fired.

Next on Fargo's agenda was dragging the dead coyotes from the basin and rolling them into a gully far enough away to be spared the smell their rotting bodies would soon give off. By then the Ovaro had grazed its fill, and he guided it into a stand of brush and slender saplings on the southwest edge of the basin. Soon, he hoped, it would be his turn to fill his belly.

Rifle across his lap, Fargo sat cross-legged and focused on a game trail that wound into the basin from the east. Gradually, the shadows deepened. Night was almost upon them, and with it came a slight but welcome breeze.

Fargo sat motionless, his stomach rumbling every now

and then. The clink of small hooves alerted him that the moment he was waiting for had arrived. Over the top of the basin filed four deer, three does and a buck—the buck was in the lead. Halfway to the spring, it halted and sniffed. Either it had caught the coyotes' scent, or Fargo's, or both. It surveyed the basin but didn't spot Fargo or the stallion. Regaining confidence, it came lower.

Fargo slowly tucked the Henry's stock to his shoulder. He already had a cartridge in the chamber. Taking precise aim at a point where the slug would pierce the buck's heart, he held his breath to steady his aim, and fired. At the Henry's boom, the buck vaulted high into the air. It managed to take two long bounds before it collapsed.

The does whirled at the shot and disappeared in full flight over the rim. Fargo let them go. He had enough meat now to last, as soon as he was done properly preparing it. The task could wait until morning, though. Of more immediate concern was his empty stomach.

Carving the buck up took more time than Fargo anticipated, thanks to his condition, but at last he had it skinned and a sizeable haunch roasting over a cozy fire. His mouth wouldn't stop watering, and he was constantly jabbing his toothpick into the juicy flesh to see if it was done enough. Ordinarily, he liked his venison roasted through and through, but tonight he settled for a few shades past rare.

Meat had seldom tasted so good. Or so Fargo thought as he tore into the haunch with wolfish gusto. He remembered to chew before swallowing or risk being sick, and each time some slid down his throat, he grinned to beat blue blazes. Making a pig of himself, he devoured more than he could recall ever eating at one sitting. Then, leaning back, he contentedly patted his gut and reflected on the fact there might be some truth to the old saying about the way to a man's heart was through his stomach. He'd always favored the notion it was through a man's pants.

Chuckling, Fargo roused himself and put coffee on to brew. He was glad he hadn't lost his coffee pot. It had been with him nearly as long as the Ovaro and had the dents and dings to prove it.

The advent of night brought with it the sounds of wild animals that preferred darkness over daylight. In the distance coyotes yipped. Periodically, a roving mountain lion screeched to attract a mate. More deer visited the basin but were too timid to enter. Fargo saw their eyes mirrored in the firelight. They would watch him a while and leave, bound he suspected, for another watering hole.

The sound that interested Fargo the most, though, came about midnight. He had fallen asleep next to the crackling fire, and as tired as he was, he expected to sleep the whole night long. When his sore eyes slid painfully open, he rose onto an elbow and tried to determine what had awakened him.

The night seemed tranquil, but appearances were more often than not deceiving. Fargo heard the hoot of an owl from among the junipers, and the chirping of crickets. Then, as he was about to lie back down, he heard the faint sound of what might be a barking dog.

Puzzled, Fargo sat straighter. He had to be mistaken. It must be a coyote. There weren't any dogs within a hundred miles. But as the barking continued he had to admit it certainly did sound like one. It was somewhere to the south, deep in the depths of the unexplored range.

Fargo lay back down, cupped his hands under his head, and searched his memory for any recollection of a settlement in that region. To the best of his knowledge there wasn't one, and never had been. Yet where there were dogs, inevitably there were people.

Still pondering the mystery, Fargo fell asleep. His final thought before he drifted off was that when next he opened his eyes, the sun would be up. But he was wrong.

It seemed as if mere seconds had elapsed, when in fact it was the middle of the night when Fargo woke up a second time. Again he had the conviction something had awakened him. He lay quietly, listening for the dog, and heard instead the stealthy pad of footsteps.

In sheer reflex Fargo shot upright, flourishing the Colt

21

as he rose. Across the basin something moved. Something big, but hunched down low. A bear, Fargo assumed, until the prowler rose on what appeared to be two legs and darted over the rim with a peculiar rolling gait.

Goose bumps crawled down Fargo's skin. Whatever it was—whoever it was—moved with astounding speed. Bears couldn't move that fast on two legs so it had to be a man. But no self-respecting Ute would be caught alone in the middle of the desert in the dead of night, and no white man in his right mind would stray that far from the trail to Oregon.

What was it, then? Hunkering, Fargo rekindled the fire. Once he had it going, he replaced his Colt, snatched up the Henry, selected a burning brand, and warily approached the opposite rim.

There were tracks, sure enough, but unlike any Fargo ever seen. Huge, oval footprints, with no evidence of toes or heels. They lent the impression that the thing walked on giant stumps. Bending closer, Fargo saw tiny fine lines where hairs had brushed the dust, leading him to deduce his visitor wore pieces of hide wrapped around both feet. It made for crude if serviceable footwear. The burning question to be answered: who wore them? Utes favored moccasins, whites preferred boots or shoes.

Fargo held the brand over his head and peered intently into the night. He had an uneasy feeling that he was being watched. Backing down the slope, he crossed to the fire and sat with his back to the cliff. Whoever was out there had to come to him, not the other way around. It would be foolhardy to venture into the darkness. He would be easy prey. His eyes were still swollen and unreliable, and his body was still feeling the effects of the brutal punishment he had endured.

Fargo heaped more wood on the fire and the ring of light expanded. Silhouetted in its glare on the far rim was the same hunched shape as before. Fargo brought up the Henry but again the figure melted into the darkness in the blink of an eye. And again without making the slightest sound.

Cradling the Henry with his finger on the trigger, Fargo waited for the nocturnal prowler to return. If it was an Ute out for blood, odds were the warrior wouldn't make his move before sunrise, which was hours away.

As time progressed, Fargo had trouble keeping his eyes open. Any other night, he would rely on the Ovaro's sharp ears and nose to warn him of danger. But in the stallion's current condition, it wouldn't wake up if the mountain came tumbling down on top of them.

Struggle as he might, Fargo drifted off. Presently a noise awakened him and he snapped his head up, but no one was there. It was a pattern he was to repeat a dozen times over the next couple of hours, compounding his weariness. After what seemed like an eternity, a rosy band framed the eastern horizon, heralding the dawn. With the hope that the sun would bring relative safety, Fargo curled onto his side, his arm for a pillow, and was adrift in heavy slumber within moments. He dreamed of creatures with fangs and claws and talons.

Heat on Fargo's face returned him to the here and now. It was early afternoon, and the basin was sweltering. His buckskins were stuck to his skin, and his eyes were throbbing. Sluggishly rising, he dipped his tin cup in the spring. It restored enough vitality for him to see how the Ovaro was faring.

The stallion wasn't much better. Less puss was leaking from its eyes, but the swelling hadn't gone down all that much. Fargo washed them both off, then applied more mud. Guiding the pinto to a spot of shade, he turned his attention to the remains of the buck he had slain. After cutting the meat into thin strips, he draped them over a bush to dry out. The meat wouldn't last as long as salted jerky, but long enough to help restore him to some semblance of his former self.

Munching on a thick slice, Fargo walked to where he had found the tracks of the phantom skulker. They led him to a boulder and from there to a vantage point only a few yards from the rim. Whoever it was had spied on him a while, then loped around the basin and gone off to the south. Interestingly enough, that was the direction the sound of the barking dog had come from. Was there a link? He wondered.

The rest of the day was spent resting and recuperating. Fargo collected grass for bedding and gathered enough firewood to last a month of Sundays. He also rounded up handfuls of dry twigs and spread them around the basin's perimeter. Anyone who tried to sneak up on him was bound to give themselves away. Lastly, Fargo looped the Ovaro's reins around his left wrist so it couldn't run off if spooked.

"That should help some," Fargo mentioned aloud. He couldn't say why, but he was certain whoever had been spying on him would be back. And this time they might have more than spying in mind.

Another supper of roast venison washed down with leftover coffee, had Fargo feeling content and rejuvenated. The setting sun blazed the western third of the sky in vivid bands of red, orange, and yellow, which slowly faded to grey. Stars blossomed, celestial flowers painted on a coal canvas. On cue, coyotes raised a canine refrain. In answer, from out of the mountains' furthermost recesses, echoed the barking of the dog.

Fargo built up the campfire more than he typically would, reminding him of an Indian expression to the effect that white men always made their fires too big and paid for their mistake with the loss of their scalps. But he wasn't too concerned. A fire at the bottom of the basin couldn't be seen from any great distance, which, in itself was food for thought. Whoever had been skulking around the previous night must have been there for a specific reason. Maybe they were after water. Or game.

Time passed, and drowsiness set in. Fargo's chin dipped to his chest and he closed his eyes. He thought of the dog, his curiosity piqued. It might be worth investigating. He would very much like to know who owned it and what they were doing there so far off the beaten path.

Sleep claimed him, and it was well that Fargo had spread the dry twigs along the rim, for a loud *crunch* snapped him bolt upright. He spied the same large, hulking figure from the night before, staring down at him from above. "Who are you?" he hollered. "What do you want?"

No reply was forthcoming.

Fargo took a step and hiked the Henry. A guttural growl was flung at him, a growl more beastlike than human. The thing was on all fours this time and, exhibiting speed that rivaled a cougar's, it spun and was gone.

Fargo had never seen the like. Now he wasn't sure *what* it was. He had caught a glimpse of fur, yet he had also glimpsed extremely pale skin. And the size of the thing! Squatting, he poured himself more coffee. As much as he needed rest, he couldn't afford to let down his guard.

During the whole incident, the Ovaro hadn't so much as twitched a muscle. It wasn't a good sign. Somehow, Fargo must find a medicinal plant to stem the infection even if it meant scouring every square foot of Utah Territory.

Placing the Henry beside him, Fargo listened for a sign the lurker was still nearby. Half an hour dragged by, and he had about convinced himself the thing was gone when a slew of stones clattered down from high atop the cliff, spilling to earth an arm's-length from where he sat.

Leaping up, Fargo trained the Henry on the cliff rim sixty feet above. A darkling form was in motion, almost invisible in the greater darkness of the night. He snapped off a shot, heard the slug whine off rock, and mentally swore at himself for not taking a moment to aim. The form faded from view as silently as a specter.

Fargo's heart hammered in his chest. He wasn't one to spook easy but this had him rattled. The stones that fell might have saved his life. The thing could well have sent a boulder plummeting down on top of him, crushing him where he sat. But maybe he was jumping to the wrong conclusion. So far it had made no attempt to harm him.

Edging to the left, Fargo moved toward the end of the cliff. There must be a game trail to the top. That was how the thing got up there, and that was how it must come back down. As likely a spot as any for him to wait and spring a little surprise of his own.

Fargo ascended the basin slope, planting each foot quietly before moving the next. Once over the rim, he no longer had the benefit of the firelight. Gloom shrouded him as he rounded the cliff and scanned the face for a way up. And there it was, a narrow ledge winding toward the craggy heights.

Fargo smiled. He had outfoxed whoever or whatever he was up against. When it reached the bottom, he would be there to greet it at gunpoint.

Suddenly the night was split by a terror-spawned whinny. Hooves drummed in wild cadence. Whirling, Fargo raced back around the cliff and down into the basin. He realized that he was the one who had been outfoxed. Either the lurker had an accomplice, or there was another way down from the top.

In the dancing glow of the fire, Fargo had his worst fear confirmed.

The Ovaro was gone.

3

The sun beat brutally down on the mountain range that had no name.

Alone amid an ocean of scorched stone broken by islands of vegetation, Skye Fargo hiked southward, his eyes glued to the tracks he had been following since first light. In his left hand was the Henry. A box of ammunition for it bulged from his pants pocket. His buckskins were drenched with sweat, as was the red bandanna around his forehead. His eyes were bothering him and his lips hurt like hell. He was tired and achey, and about stove in, but he would be damned if he would let anything turn him from his task. He would reclaim the Ovaro or he would die trying.

Whoever had been stalking him—and Fargo was convinced it was a person, not an animal—had deliberately dropped those stones from the top of the cliff to lure him away from the stallion. Then the horse thief had descended by a different route, grabbed the pinto's reins, and hastened to the south.

The thought of it seared Fargo like a red-hot ember. The Ovaro was near-blind, weak, and helpless. It had depended on him and he had let it down. He had fallen for a ruse only a rank greenhorn would fall for.

Fargo's anger helped sustain him. It lent him extra energy to go on when his legs flagged. It fueled his resolve not to rest until he had dealt out his own personal brand of justice to the bastard responsible. And deal it out he would. He couldn't wait to get the thief in his gun sights.

It was close to noon and the heat was stifling. Oppressive heat waves rose off the ground like burn from a flame. Fargo tried not to think of the spring, of the last long drink he had savored before heading out. His saddle and other effects were secreted in the underbrush and should be safe enough until he returned to the basin.

A shadow rippled across him, and Fargo glanced up. His old friends, the buzzards, were back, circling and trying to assess whether he would collapse any time soon. "Forget it!" he snarled. "Find yourself another meal!"

As if they understood, the big black birds banked on the currents and flew off in search of a likelier prospect.

A rocky sawtooth rise appeared. Fargo climbed laboriously, his feet melting in his boots. He wondered if the horse thief had traveled all night, for if so he had a long and taxing journey ahead. In one regard he had been lucky. The thief was still leading the Ovaro instead of riding it. Which puzzled him. Why steal the stallion if not to ride it? What else did the thief have in mind?

Fargo came to the crest and halted. Below was a secluded belt of vegetation hemmed by stone peaks. Grass grew in profusion, and trees lined a narrow creek. But what sent a tingle of anticipation down his spine was a man-made structure, a small cabin situated near the creek, flanked by a corral.

In the corral was the Ovaro.

Fargo's first impulse was to run down and yell for the owner of the cabin to step outside or he would riddle it with bullets. But he hadn't lasted as long as he had by being rash. Crouching, he worked his way to an arroyo that would bring him within a bow shot of the homestead. He had only gone a short way when he discovered more tracks. Older tracks. The huge, oval prints of the thief. Evidently, whoever had stolen the pinto had lived there quite a while.

Smoke curled from a stone chimney. Someone was cooking a meal. The cabin wasn't made of logs but from old planks badly in need of paint and repair. Whoever built it wasn't very handy with tools. Some of the planks overlapped and others were at odd angles, and the ends had been sawed unevenly. A plank door faced the creek. On the same side was a small window adorned by burlap curtains.

From the arroyo, Fargo threaded through the trees until he was close to the rear, and the corral. The Ovaro was in shade by the cabin. Since there were no doors or windows on this side, Fargo felt safe in cat-footing to the gate, which consisted of two trimmed saplings set into slots, and removing them.

"It's me, fella," Fargo whispered to forestall a whinny.

The thief was taking extraordinarily decent care of the pinto. A cloth bandage covered its eyes and ointment coated the raw areas on its back and flanks. A mound of grass had been heaped in a corner next to a full water trough. It had all the comforts of a stable.

"I've done the best I could, mister. I hope it's enough."

At the sound of the voice, Fargo spun. He leveled the Henry, his thumb on the hammer, before it hit him the speaker was a woman.

She stood at the far corner of the cabin, her full figure sheathed in a homespun dress that had seen better years. A clean apron was around her waist, and she held a large wooden spoon. Her face, framed by lustrous blonde hair, was lovely enough to turn heads on any street corner. She had frank green eyes that regarded him without any trace of fear or anxiety. Her red lips curving in a smile, she came to the rails. "I'm sorry if I've startled you. I'm Sarah Arvin. I live here."

Fargo warily moved toward her. She seemed harmless enough, but he held the Henry on her anyway. "By yourself?" he asked.

Arvin hesitated. "Yes. Alone. Is that your horse? It wandered in here early this morning all by itself."

"Did it, now?" Fargo sarcastically responded. Her lie proved he did well not trusting her. Maybe the thief was her husband. The man could be close by, waiting to pounce.

"You sound as if you don't believe me, Mr.—?"

"Fargo." He glanced behind him, then at the trees. "And we both know why that is, don't we?"

Sadness crept into Sarah Arvin's eyes and tone. "I'm sorry. I was hoping you didn't know about him. He can move like a ghost when he wants to."

"Ghosts don't leave tracks," Fargo said. "And his led me right to your doorstep. You have some explaining to do, lady. Who stole my horse? In case he hasn't heard, it's a hanging offense in some parts."

Sarah blanched. "Please. Let's not bring up that. I can assure you that he meant you no harm. Why, he wouldn't harm a flea."

"Who is this 'he' we're talking about?"

The blonde opened her mouth to answer, then suddenly took a step back in dismay, and raising an arm, she cried out, "No, Clarence! No!"

Clarence? Fargo started to turn but he was too late. Enormous arms corded with muscle looped around him from behind and constricted like twin pythons. He was lifted and shaken as a terrier might shake a mouse. The Henry went flying. Fetid breath filled his nose, and a familiar guttural growl filled his ears. The pressure on his ribs was unbelievable. He felt them buckling, felt them on the verge of being shattered. Driving his head back, he slammed it into the face of his assailant. A feral howl greeted his gambit.

"Clarence! Drop him this instant!"

The arms binding him relaxed and Fargo was unceremoniously dumped to the dirt. Rolling over, he stabbed his hand for the Colt, then froze.

The monstrosity looming over him was something out of a madman's fevered imagination. It stood over seven feet in height, with shoulders to rival a bear's. A crudely cured deer hide covered a torso as broad around as a barrel. Both arms and legs were unnaturally pale, as was its hideous face. The left eye was an inch higher than the right, the left half of its crooked nose twice the size of the other half. A twisted caricature of a mouth, rimmed by large teeth, dribbled drool.

"Clarence!" Sarah repeated. "You're not to harm him, you hear? He's only after his horse! He's not out to hurt us."

Bobbing his double chin, Clarence backed off. For some reason he was constantly squinting. He gently placed a ham-sized hand on the Ovaro, and uttering inarticulate gibberish, rubbed the pinto's back. A grin, or some semblance of one, creased his horrid countenance.

Sarah hastened around to the gate and entered as Fargo slowly picked himself up. "He'd never harm your horse, mister. He'd never harm any animal. He can't stand to see them suffer. That's why he brought it here for me to doctor."

"For you to doctor?" Fargo watched the man-brute affectionately rub behind the Ovaro's ear and then give the stallion a hug. It was hard to judge Clarence's age, but Fargo had the impression the giant was young, in his mid- to late teens. Sarah appeared to be in her early to midthirties, possibly a little older. "Is he your son?" was the logical conclusion.

"He's my link to the underground. I look after him and feed him and he watches over me and protects me."

She had avoided the question, Fargo noted. "Protects you from who? And what do you mean by 'underground'?"

Sighing, Sarah clasped her slender hands. "There's so much to explain, I wouldn't know where to begin." She walked up and touched his arm. "I'd rather discuss you. You're not one of Vrittan's bunch so you must be from the outside world." Sarah stepped to the Ovaro. "And you've brought a horse! A magnificent, wonderful horse!"

"A person might think you've never seen one before," Fargo quipped.

"Not in years," Sarah said, placing her hand on the pinto in almost reverent awe. "If I had, do you think I would still be here? Not on your life." Tears welled in her eyes, and her throat bobbed a few times. "You don't realize it, but you're my salvation. The answer to all my prayers."

31

Too much was being thrown at Fargo too fast. "We need to sit down and talk, lady," he advised. Plus, he was hoping she would see fit to offer him some water and food.

"Where are my manners? You look as if you've been through the wringer, and here I am prattling like an idiot. Please forgive me. Come inside and rest. Can I offer you any refreshment? Are you hungry?"

"I could eat my horse whole," Fargo joked. To his considerable amazement, she took him seriously.

"Don't you dare!" Sarah threw an arm over the stallion, acting like a brood hen defending a chick. "There's not a lot of game hereabouts, but enough for us to get by. I have some rabbit stew on right this moment, in fact. More than plenty for the three of us. You're welcome to as much as you can eat."

Fargo picked up the Henry. "I'd be obliged," he said, wiping the dust off. "I haven't had home-cooked food in more days than I care to recollect."

Gripping Clarence's elbow to get his attention, Sarah looked him right in the eyes and said, "Stay close and watch over the horse. If anyone comes anywhere near my place, you're to let me know right away. Do you understand?"

The young brute grunted.

"You're such a dear," Sarah said, stroking his cheek, and Clarence lit up like a lantern. "I could never have lasted as long as I have without you. If only the rest were the same." Her face clouding, Sarah beckoned to Fargo and escorted him around to the front of her cabin. The plank door hung open. She stepped to one side so he could precede her, but he held back.

"Ladies first, ma'am."

"I like a man with manners," Sarah commented light-heartedly. Her dress swishing, she slid past him.

For a second their bodies were inches apart. Her hair smelled of minty pine, and her body had the scrubbed aroma of lye soap. Fargo couldn't help but admire the swell of her bosom and the enticing sway to her hips. She was a beautiful woman. In places like St. Louis and

New Orleans she would be the toast of the city. What she was doing here was beyond him.

The interior of the cabin was as plainly furnished as a monastery. A table with two chairs occupied the main room, and along one wall was a rough-hewn counter. The plank floor was pitted and scraped. From a rusted tripod in a shoddy stone fireplace hung a rusted kettle in which the stew bubbled. Through an adjoining doorway a bed was visible. Some would call the cabin a hovel. But it was apparent Sarah Arvin took pride in her home. The floor was clean enough to eat off of, the furniture and the counter were free of dust and dirt. A faded painting of a yellow flower, and a worn blanket used as a rug added a touch of elementary elegance.

"It's not much but it's all I have," Sarah was saying. Opening a cupboard, she rummaged inside. "I recall having a smidgen of coffee left. I was saving it for a special occasion, and this surely qualifies. It isn't often I have company." She added offhandedly, "Other than Clarence, that is."

Fargo shifted one of the chairs so he could see the front door and the window, both. Depositing his Henry on the table, he sat down. "No need to go to any trouble on my account. Water will do fine."

"Indulge me, Mr. Fargo," Sarah said. "You can't begin to appreciate how much your visit means to me." She brought out an old can of Arbuckle's. "Ah. Here it is. Give me a few minutes and you'll have a meal fit for a king." She smiled warmly.

"Suppose you tell me a little about yourself and how you got here," Fargo prompted.

"I'm from Illinois," Sarah began as she removed a coffee pot from a cupboard above the counter. "I was part of the Kimmel wagon train that came west in '49, bound for the gold fields of California. Forty wagons in all. Mostly families with kids." She pulled the lid off the pot, then frowned. "We never made it out of Utah Territory."

"Indians?"

"No, nothing like that. We made camp one night along

33

the trail well north of here. Shortly after supper, a man by the name of Charlie Vrittan hailed our camp, and the wagon boss let him join us. My husband and I took Vrittan for a typical prospector, but we couldn't have been more wrong. He's the Devil incarnate."

Fargo glanced toward the bedroom. "Your husband?"

"Long since dead. But I'll get to him shortly." Sarah poured water from a bucket on the counter into the pot. "Vrittan inquired where we were bound and we told him. He asked us why we wanted to travel so far when there was more pure yellow ore than any of us could spend in a lifetime within a few days' ride."

"Gold in these parts?" Fargo knew of no such gold strikes. Had there been, word would have spread faster than a prairie fire, resulting in another gold rush.

Sarah motioned at the window. "In these mountains, Mr. Fargo. Or, to be more precise, under them. The main strike was near the town of Vrittan."

"There's a town named after him?" Fargo leaned back, his gaze roving over the fine contours of her backside. She could do a man proud, that one, and remind him of why he *was* a man. "You're getting ahead of yourself."

"Bear with me. You see, back then Vrittan had a grand plan. He'd struck it rich, but he couldn't transport all the ore out by his lonesome. It would take a century. He needed help, but he wanted to keep his strike secret so hordes of gold seekers wouldn't come swarming in from all over creation."

"Yet he told everyone on your wagon train? With that many wagons, there must have been over a hundred people."

"One hundred and thirty-seven, to be exact. Many were children. Clarence was only six at the time. His parents were taking him West hoping to get a new start somewhere he wouldn't be teased on account of his looks." Sarah paused. "Anyway, back to Vrittan. He had a proposition. He wanted us to settle in these mountains instead of going on to California. In exchange for our help in mining the ore, he'd let us have a stake in his claim."

To Fargo it didn't sound right. "Awful generous of him. Offering a fortune to people he hardly knew."

"He had it all thought out. Vrittan knew that once word spread, a town would spring up. They always do at gold strikes. Swarms of greedy vultures would swoop in, and maybe push him off his claim."

It had happened before, Fargo reflected. Too many times to count. Vigilance committees were often set up specifically to deal with claim jumpers.

"Vrittan wasn't about to have his find stolen out from under him. As part of the conditions he laid down, he made us promise to look out for his interests at all times."

"And since he was sharing his gold, his interests became your interests," Fargo interrupted.

"Exactly," Sarah said, nodding. "Another condition was that we name the town after him. He was most insistent on that. I never did learn why."

"Did you learn why he picked your wagon train over all the others that must have gone by?"

"Yes, as a matter of fact. It was all our children. He felt safer approaching a train of family folk. We were less apt to turn on him and force him to reveal where his claim was, or so he told me later."

From the sound of things, Fargo mused, Charlie Vrittan was a savvy sage rat. "I take it everyone agreed?"

Sarah faced him. "You must understand. Most of us were dirt poor and had barely scraped up enough money for the journey. We were all hoping to strike it rich in California, but there were no guarantees. And then along came this little man who offered us a decent share of his find, and all we had to do was settled here in these mountains and lend him a hand." She gave a shudder. "How were we to foresee things would go so horribly wrong? That so many would lose their lives?"

"Things didn't work out?"

Sarah seemed not to hear him. "Mr. Clydell was the first. He was our wagon boss. He didn't trust Vrittan, and he argued against our going. When we took a vote and it was unanimous, he said he would go with us just to make sure we got there in one piece. The very night we arrived, he went to check on the horses and was never seen again. Vrittan claimed Utes were to blame. But I should have known better. I should have—"

Feet pounded outside and someone hammered on the door so hard, it was nearly torn from its leather hinges. Fargo rose and scooped up the Henry as Sarah rushed to open it.

Clarence's bulk nearly filled the doorway. Gesturing to the south, he mouthed grunts and gurgles that made no sense to Fargo.

"He's trying to tell us someone is coming," Sarah said. "The way he's acting, it must be some of Vrittan's crowd." She turned and ran to the blanket that lay on the floor just beyond the table. Bending, she yanked it off, revealing a trapdoor which she swiftly opened. Under the cabin was a root cellar, a ladder propped against one side.

Without being bid, Clarence lumbered to the opening and squeezed his gigantic frame on through. Grinning lopsidedly at Sarah, he descended.

"Now you," Sarah said, looking at Fargo.

Fargo didn't much like the notion of being cooped up with the giant for who-knew-how-long. "No thanks. I'll stay up here with you."

"It's too dangerous. Vrittan's men will want to drag you into town. And they'll confiscate your horse."

That settled it. Fargo moved toward the front door, saying, "I already had my stallion taken once. It's not going to happen again. I'll lead him into the trees and lay low until your visitors are gone."

Sarah lowered the trapdoor and replaced the blanket. "I can see there is no arguing with you. So hurry. They might have already spotted the pinto."

Fargo was out the door in a twinkling. He glanced southward, but saw no one. Sprinting to the corral, he quickly and carefully slipped his bridle on the pinto and guided it out the gate, heading due west. But he hadn't gone ten yards when four figures emerged from the forest bordering the creek.

"You there! Mister! Hold on!"

The quartet hustled across the clearing. They were a motley group, their clothes dirty and torn, their grimy, bearded faces in dire need of a scrubbing. Two wore revolvers, the others carried older-model rifles.

Fargo kept walking, the Henry against his right leg. He could better protect the stallion in the trees. But the foursome swiftly overtook him and planted themselves in front of him. Halting, he didn't mince words. "You're in my way. Move."

The tallest hooked his thumbs in his gunbelt and declared. "Didn't you hear me? I said to hold up. We need to talk."

"And didn't you hear me?" Fargo asked, pointing the Henry at the tall drink of water's stomach.

The man's chest deflated like a punctured bubble. "Now you hold on, there, stranger! Don't you have any notion who we are?"

One of the others, a stocky fellow with a big nose and a Sharps, snapped, "How the hell would he know about all that's going on? Use your head, Moran. He's an outsider." The man repeated the word softly, as if in awe. "An *outsider*."

Moran couldn't take his beady eyes off the Henry's muzzle. "I don't care who he is, Bokor! No one points a gun at us." He glared at Fargo. "Listen, stranger, and listen good. You don't want to get us riled. Give us trouble and there will be hell to pay."

"Is it your ears?" Fargo asked.

"Huh?" Moran wasn't the brightest lamp in the world. "What do my ears have to do with anything?"

"They must be plugged with wax," Fargo said. "Didn't you hear me tell you to get out of my way?"

"Sure I heard you, but—"

Fargo had given the man his chance. Moran appeared to believe he had the God-given right to ride roughshod over everyone as he saw fit, and it was high time someone showed him that wasn't the case. The West was full of hardcases like him, idiots who were always on the prod, jackasses who only learned better when they had it pounded into their thick skulls. Twisting at the waist, he drove the Henry's barrel into the pit of Moran's gut, then trained the rifle on the others as Moran collapsed like a house of cards and lay sputtering and gasping in the dirt. "Anyone else who can't hear?"

Bokor held his arms out from his sides to show he wasn't about to try something stupid. "We heard you, mister. And we'll leave you be. But it won't hurt to listen to what I have to say, will it?"

"Make it quick."

"About five miles south of here is a town. Trust me when I say it would be well worth your while to pay it a visit. We haven't had an outsider here in a coon's age, and Mr. Vrittan will be mighty interested in making your acquaintance."

"Never heard of the man," Fargo feigned ignorance. "And as soon as my horse mends, I'm moving on."

Bokor glanced at the Ovaro. "I hadn't noticed. Your critter is in pretty bad shape." His brown eyes darted to the cabin. "I take it you're resting up here, is that it? Which means you'll be sticking around a while." He smiled amiably enough. "Good. We'll be on our way, then. I hope there are no hard feelings, and that you'll pay Mr. Vrittan a visit real soon. It's for your own benefit."

"Let me be the judge of that." Fargo covered them as Moran was boosted to his feet and the four backed off. They made no attempt to resort to their hardware. But just in case, he stayed where he was and watched them thread through the trees to a hill beyond the creek, well out of rifle range. Lowering the Henry, he turned.

Sarah Arvin was approaching. "I saw everything from my window. I wish you had gone into the root cellar like I wanted."

"All I did was teach them some manners."

"I'm afraid you've done far worse. They'll tell Charlie Vrittan about you, and he'll want your head on a platter." Sarah sadly shook her head. "And now mine as well."

4

The first spoonful of rabbit stew banished all other considerations but food from Skye Fargo's mind. He hadn't realized how famished he was, and couldn't ladle it into his mouth fast enough. Beside the bowl were two thick slabs of homemade bread that he dipped into the broth and chewed lustily. Closing his eyes, he groaned in rapture.

Sarah Arvin laughed. "I appreciate the compliment, kind sir, but it's not *that* good. I've been out of salt for months, and the few seasonings I have left don't amount to much."

"You could have fooled me," Fargo responded.

"Eat to your heart's content, then. I always make enough to last several days. The less cooking I have to do, the better." Sarah removed her apron and stepped to the chair across from him. "Like most women, I'm lazy when it comes to kitchen work." She started to sit down, then snapped her fingers and exclaimed, "Where is my mind today? I almost forgot."

Fargo scooped more stew into his mouth as she scooted to the rug, tossed it aside, and opened the trapdoor.

"Clarence! You can come up now! Our meal is ready."

Fargo stared at the square opening, expecting the great, deformed head to rear up. But it didn't, and Sarah lowered the trapdoor, showing no concern whatsoever. "Did he leave while we were outside?"

"Yes, but not how you think."

Fargo was going to ask what she meant, but she

abruptly dashed to the hearth. The coffee pot was bubbling over. She had left it on too long. After wrapping a washcloth around her hand, she snatched the pot from near the flames and carried it to the counter.

"Honestly, sometimes I wonder where my brains are."

"I'm still waiting to hear what happened after your wagon boss disappeared," Fargo remarked.

While she fetched a cup and filled it, Sarah related, "From the outset nothing went like it was supposed to. Charlie Vrittan wouldn't show us where he made his strike. Not until the town was built, he said. So we pitched together and put up enough buildings to satisfy him. But he still wouldn't show us. When some of the men complained he wasn't holding up his end of the bargain, my husband among them, Vrittan went off back among the peaks and came back three days later with a poke chock full of nuggets as big as your knuckles."

"Would he say where he found them?"

"No. After all the trouble he went to in order to bring us here, at the last minute Charlie changed his mind about sharing. He was afraid some of us would jump his claim."

"You should have left then and there," Fargo said.

"We tried. We took a vote and it was unanimous. We decided to go the next morning, and everyone went to pack their wagons. But that night the Utes struck and made off with all our stock. Every horse. Every ox. Every mule." Sarah brought over a piping-hot cup and bent to carefully place it next to his elbow.

Again Fargo inhaled the minty fragrance of her hair. Her ripe body, so close, so tantalizing, triggered a twitching in his groin. "Are you sure Utes were to blame?"

'Some of us wondered. We never found any Indian sign. But there was no way Charlie could have driven off all our stock by his lonesome. Not over two hundred head."

Fargo wasn't so sure. By breaking the herd down into manageable numbers, one man could move that many in one night.

"We've been stranded in these desolate mountains ever since," Sarah said. "Those of us still alive, at any rate."

"You've been here eleven years?" Fargo marveled. "Why didn't someone go for help?"

"Several tried. But they must not have made it because help never came." Sarah sank into her chair and leaned forward on her forearms. It caused her more than ample breasts to push against the thin fabric of her dress, accenting their contours. "Either the desert got them, or the Utes did. Either way, no one has had the grit to try in ages. So here we sit, the Dirt Breathers and the Air Breathers, whittling ourselves down until there won't be anyone left."

Fargo had momentarily forgotten about his soup. "The what breathers?"

"Sorry. Those are the nicknames the two sides call one another." Sarah folded her arms across her bosom. "Long ago we split into factions. One group hated Vrittan for misleading us and refused to have anything more to do with him. The other group felt obligated to stick with him and make the best of things." Her luscious lips formed into a pout. "Those men you met earlier, Moran and Bokor and the rest? They're from the wagon train, just like me. Only where I hate Charlie, they lick his boots. They, and the rest of the Air Breathers."

"Why are they called that?"

"I don't rightly remember who started it. Charlie and the rest who live in town are called Air Breathers. The other group, those who oppose him, live down in the old mine tunnels, and they're called Dirt Breathers. They took shelter there after the fighting broke out. Now it's a stalemate, with neither side able to whip the other."

Fargo began to better understand the situation, but her account raised as many questions as it answered. "Where did these tunnels come from?"

Sarah ran a hand through her luxuriant golden mane and absently stared at the window. A sunbeam lit up her fair complexion, highlighting the smooth, creamy texture of her skin and the cherry red of her luscious lips.

"You're aware, I'd wager, that back when Spain controlled much of the southwest, the Spanish had gold mines scattered all over."

Fargo nodded. Spanish gold diggings had been found as far north as Colorado. But none, to his knowledge, in Utah Territory.

"These mountains were the site of an old Spanish mine. We learned about it when one of the children stumbled on an entrance near town."

"Was that where Vrittan got his gold?" Fargo probed.

"Charlie swore he never knew the tunnels were there, and that his strike was elsewhere." Sarah sipped her coffee. "Not that it matters anymore. Most of us just want to escape this madness. We've been praying for someone from the outside world to find us. Someone just like you." She gazed into his eyes. "Our lives are in your hands. As soon as that stallion of yours is fit enough, get on him and ride like the wind to the nearest army post. Tell them where to find us." She slid her hand across the table and enfolded his wrist. "Save us, Mr. Fargo. Save *me*. I don't know how much more of this I can take. How much more bloodshed. How much more fear." Her fingernails bit into his flesh. "How much more loneliness."

Fargo had no objection to letting the military know what was going on. Nor to leading a patrol back there personally. He mentioned as much to Sarah and her grip relaxed.

"It would mean the world to me. I don't know how I could ever repay your kindness. Ask of me what you will and it's yours."

Was it Fargo's imagination or was she offering more than mere hospitality? His rumbling stomach diverted his interest and he polished off two heaping bowls of stew and washed it all down with half a pot of coffee. Then he sat back, as refreshed and well fed as he had been in weeks. Only one thing would make it complete. He envisioned the charms under Sarah Arvin's dress, and daydreamed.

Sarah had fallen silent while they ate. Now she, too,

finished and after taking the dirty bowls over to the counter, sat back down and took up where she had left off. "Of the original one hundred and thirty-seven emigrants on the wagon train, about seventy-five are left, give or take a few. A dozen died trying to reach civilization. Some were taken by Utes. Most, though, have been casualties of the unending war the two factions are waging."

"They're killing one another off?"

"You must understand. The Dirt Breathers and the Air Breathers hate one another. They each blame the other for our plight. Vrittan would dearly love to wipe the Dirt Breathers out, but his men are afraid to go into the tunnels where they live for fear of booby traps. They've lost quite a few that way."

The whole affair sounded insane to Fargo. The two sides needed to work together, not fight each other.

A strange laugh fluttered from Sarah's throat. "The Dirt Breathers have been underground for so long, they usually only come out at night now."

"What about you? Whose side are you on?"

"I've tried to remain neutral, to be the voice of reason, but I must confess I'm not partial to Charlie Vrittan. Those men today came to fetch me. Vrittan has long been badgering me to take up his housekeeping, as he puts it. But I refuse. I haven't been with a man since the death of my husband, and I'll be damned if I'll sleep with a worm like him. No matter how lonely I am," she emphatically concluded.

Fargo cleared his throat. "If you don't mind my asking, how exactly did your husband die? And where are your kids?"

Sarah's eyes misted and it was a while before she answered. "My husband, Frank, was one of those who tried to go for help. We only had one child, our son, Maxwell, who was twelve when Frank set out. Frank made Max promise to look after me until he got back, but that first night after Frank left, while I was asleep, Max snuck out and lit out after his father." A tear trickled down each cheek. "They never returned. I know they're dead. Either the desert or the Utes got them."

"I'm sorry."

Sarah exhaled and squared her shoulders. "Enough about me." She grinned half-heartedly. "Tell me about you. What do you do and why are you here?"

Fargo mentioned the scouting he sometimes did for the army. He did a lot of other work, everything from guiding wagon trains to searching for people lost in the wilderness, but he wasn't one to prattle.

"And you've never found the right woman and settled down? A handsome cuss like you?"

There it was again. A hint of something more in her tone. Grinning, Fargo answered honestly. "It'll be a good long while yet before I'm ready to plant roots." He locked his eyes on hers. "That doesn't mean I don't like women. There's nothing I like better than to enjoy the company of a lovely lady like yourself."

A touch of pink dappled Sarah's cheeks. "My, my, aren't you the gallant gentleman?" She smiled a tad nervously. "But I will admit I like your company as well. It's been far too long since I shared male companionship." Her voice dropped to a whisper laced with longing. "Far, far too long."

Fargo seized the moment. "So you don't mind if I stay the night? I won't be any bother. I can sleep out in the corral with my horse."

"Nonsense," Sarah replied. "I wouldn't hear of it. You'll sleep in here. I'll spread blankets out near the hearth and you'll be as comfortable as can be."

"Is there anything I can do to repay you for your kindness?"

Sarah's cheeks grew subtly darker. Averting her gaze, she cleared her throat and quickly stood. "While I'm doing the dishes you can gather firewood. I'll need some for cooking supper later."

"Whatever you want, ma'am," Fargo said, and ambled outside. He was looking forward to "later." If he played his cards right, it could turn out to be an extremely relaxing night.

Crossing the clearing, Fargo entered the trees. Near

the cabin there weren't any fallen branches to be found; Sarah had already used them. Hiking farther, he spotted one. The dead wood broke easily over his knee, and he was about to continue his search when something moved in the brush to his left. Pretending to scour the ground, he peered out of the corner of his eye and saw a dirt-speckled face peeking at him from the depths of a thicket.

It was one of the men who had been with Moran and Bokor. The man was alone, apparently, and although armed with a revolver, he hadn't drawn it—yet. But he would the instant he realized Fargo was on to him. Bending to pick up another branch, Fargo surreptitiously palmed his Colt. He moved a few yards nearer to the thicket, his head bent down, then suddenly straightened, dropped the firewood, and trained his Colt on the Air Breather. "Come out of there! And keep your hands where I can see them!"

The man shot to his feet, bleating, "Don't shoot, mister! Don't shoot!" He wasn't much over five feet tall and had a high, sloping forehead and fleshy jowls that trembled when he was scared. "I don't mean you no harm! Honest to God!"

Cautiously relieving him of an older model Remington, Fargo demanded, "Who are you? And what the hell are you doing back here?"

"The name's Floyd. Floyd Havershaw." Floyd stared down the Colt's barrel and licked his pudgy lips. "The truth is, I never really left. Moran had me sneak on back to keep an eye on things and make sure you didn't traipse off. That's all."

"He didn't send you to steal my horse?" Fargo asked suspiciously. Based on the information Sarah had imparted, the Ovaro was worth its weight in gold to both factions in the ongoing feud.

"No, no, not at all!" Floyd whined. "He wouldn't risk making you mad. He's counting on you to show up in town. All of us are."

"I sure wouldn't want to disappoint them." Fargo

wagged the Colt in front of Havershaw's bulbous nose. "But what am I going to do about you? Mrs. Arvin won't take kindly to you spying on her place."

"You can let me go," Floyd anxiously suggested. "I'll head straight for town and stay there. I promise."

Fargo believed him. The man was no killer. Stepping back, he nodded. "On your way, then. But if I catch you snooping around here again, the next time I might not be so charitable."

"Don't worry! I'm not hankering to die." Floyd started to sidle off, then paused. "I don't suppose you'd see fit to give my hog-leg back?"

"Don't push your luck."

"I was afraid you'd say that." Floyd darted fearful glances into the woods, then stammered, "But you see, um, that is, well." He took a deep breath. "Please, mister. Reconsider. I wouldn't expect you to understand, being an outsider and all, but there are people hereabouts who would gut me as soon as look at me. Dirt Breathers, we call 'em. They can pop up out of the ground whenever they please, and they're snake mean."

"No one can just pop out of the ground."

"The Dirt Breathers can. Their tunnels are all over the place." Floyd looked longingly at the Remington tucked under Fargo's belt. "You can unload it, if that will make you feel better."

"It won't." Fargo had no reason to trust him. Quite the contrary. "It's broad daylight. You should be safe enough." He flicked a finger to the south. "Skedaddle before I change my mind and dump you in Mrs. Arvin's root cellar for safe keeping."

"She has a cellar?" Floyd cried in stark terror, then dashed off, plowing through the undergrowth like a panicked elk.

Fargo chuckled and made for the cabin. As bad men went, Vrittan's bunch were downright pitiful. The army would have no problem rounding them up. He twirled the Colt into its holster and swerved to avoid a tree. Simultaneously, to his rear, a piercing shriek rang out. Whirling, he saw the bushes shaking and rustling fifty feet away, and thought he saw Floyd clinging to one as if for dear life.

"Help me, mister! God in heaven, help me!"

It was no act. The fear in Havershaw's voice was genuine. Drawing the Colt, Fargo raced to lend his aid as the vegetation erupted in a riot of snapping brush and desperate screams.

"They've got me! Help! Help!"

Fargo was halfway there when the sounds abruptly ceased and the undergrowth stopped moving. Rounding a last thicket, he stopped in consternation. A severely trampled patch of weeds marked the spot where Havershaw had been, and near it lay a freshly broken tree limb Floyd must have torn off in his struggles. But the man was nowhere to be seen.

"Floyd?" Fargo hollered, and warily crept forward. The woods were so still, he could hear an acorn drop. But he heard nothing, nothing at all, and that shouldn't be. Whoever attacked Floyd hadn't had time to get away. He should hear them moving off, especially if they were dragging Floyd with them. Which had to be the case. Other than the thicket, there wasn't anywhere to conceal a body.

Fargo took another step and his right foot bumped an object in the grass. It was a boot, a severely scuffed empty brown boot, that until moments ago had been on Havershaw's right foot. Fargo moved past it and swept for tracks, for broken twigs, for bent blades of grass or any other sign that would reveal in which direction they had gone. But it was as if the earth had yawned wide and swallowed Havershaw whole.

The earth. Fargo glanced down, then roved in circles, seeking evidence of a mine shaft. There was none, though. And when he stomped the ground, it appeared solid as could be. Baffled, he was making another circuit when his name was called and Sarah Arvin sashayed through the trees.

"There you are! I wondered what was keeping you so long."

Fargo related his run-in with Havershaw. "I've looked

all over but he's vanished, and I can't figure out how. There aren't any tracks."

Sarah dismissed the disappearance with a wave of her hand. "Don't concern yourself. He's one of Vrittan's men, remember? As mean a pack of curly wolves as ever wore britches."

Havershaw hadn't impressed Fargo as being particularly mean. Quite the opposite. He gave the woods a last scrutiny, then started back beside her. He had a hunch she was withholding information, but her purpose eluded him.

"You must think me very coldhearted," Sarah commented. "You wouldn't, though, if you knew all the things Vrittan and his henchmen have put me through. They're despicable, the whole outfit."

"Do you feel the same about the Dirt Breathers?"

Sarah seemed to chose her next words carefully. "I know what you're getting at. That I'm really not neutral. Yes, I favor the Dirt Breathers. But none of them have ever tried to persuade me to go to bed with them. And they don't skulk around my place at all hours of the day and night." She looked at him. "So now you know. If I could, I'd put a gun to Vrittan's head and blow his brains out. I hate the little weasel, heart and soul. Does that make my stance clear?"

"Couldn't be clearer," Fargo said.

"I'm a bitter woman," Sarah conceded. "Justifiably so, in my estimation. I lost my husband. I lost my son. All to feed a lunatic's hunger for gold ore."

"Ore he hasn't bothered to mine."

Sarah was quiet until they were at her doorstep. Then she placed a warm, velvet hand on his arm. "I don't blame you for having doubts. Nothing is ever as it appears in this world, is it?"

"Including you?"

"I'm not hiding anything, if that's what you're implying." Sarah's hand rose to his chest and her rosy lips quirked upward. "Prove it to yourself. Search me if you'd like."

There it was again. The suggestion Fargo was welcome

to do with her as he pleased. "Just remember it was your idea," he said, and covered her right breast with his hand. At the contact Sarah arched her spine, and gasped.

"Oh, my!"

"What's this?" Fargo teased. "Hiding something under your dress?" His thumb and forefinger closed on her nipple, which was growing taut through the fabric, and tweaked it, hard.

"You beast," Sarah said throatily. Thrusting herself against him, she molded her hungry mouth to his.

Fargo felt her tongue rim his lips. Her arms rose to his neck and her fingers entwined within his hair. Her hips moved in age-old rhythm, and her breath was molten lava. She craved him as much as he had craved water out on the desert. Sliding his tongue to meet hers in a moist caress, he let the kiss linger until she took it upon herself to step back and smile dreamily.

"I haven't been kissed like that in so long, I've forgotten how wonderful it is." Sarah reached behind her, opened the door, and pulled him in after her. "Shut it and throw the bolt so we're not interrupted."

Who was Fargo to argue? When he turned, she was over by the trap door, placing a chair on top of the rug covering it. "What's that for?"

"Mice," Sarah said, and giggled. In three heartbeats she was pressed against him again, her eyelids hooded in wanton urgency, her fingernails plucking at his buckskin shirt. "Don't just stand there like a bump on a log. Or do I have to undress myself?"

"First things first," Fargo said. Tucking his knees, he whisked her into his arms and strode toward the bedroom. A slight weakness in his lower legs hinted it would be days yet before he recovered, and that he'd better take things slow until then.

Sarah was running her hands over his neck and jaw. "When I called you handsome a while ago, I wasn't kidding. Compared to you, my husband was a lump of coal. God rest his soul."

Although it had been Fargo's experience wives tended to speak poorly of their husbands every chance they got, insulting a dead husband, even in jest, wasn't something most wives would deem fitting. But he didn't say anything, not with his manhood stiffening in a need too long denied.

Her bedroom was comfortably furnished with curtains and a real rug. A four-poster bend was against the opposite wall, covered by a purple quilt. Fargo carried her over to it and gently laid her down so her lustrous golden locks rested on a long pillow. Sitting next to her, he bent low over her flushed face. "No promises. You understand?"

"I wouldn't have it any other way," was Sarah's sultry reply. Tugging on his shoulders, she once again fastened her fevered lips to his and kissed him as if trying to suck him into her mouth. A groan welled in her throat when his hands covered her large twin mounds, and her left knee rose along the inside of his thigh to lightly rub his member.

Fargo grew almost as hot as he had been out on the desert. Prying at the buttons of her dress with one hand, he ran his other across her flat stomach to the junction of her legs, but no further.

"What are you waiting for, big man?" Sarah cooed.

Fargo's answer was to kiss her neck and ear. He dallied at her earlobe, which excited her immeasurably, and licked a path from her neck to the upper swell of her cleavage. By then he had unbuttoned her dress. Sliding it down low enough to reveal her undergarments, he nuzzled her breasts and inhaled the aromatic fragrance of musky perfume.

Sarah looped an arm around his head. "Oh! I like that! A lot!"

Alternating between mounds, Fargo nipped at the outlines of her nipples. She kneaded his upper arms, then lowered her right hand to sculpt the contour of his hip and thigh. He could sense she wanted to reach lower but she held back, perhaps in the belief he would think she was too aggressive. Shifting, he grasped her hand and boldly placed it on his pole.

"Oh my!" Sarah exhaled. "You could split a girl in

half." Grinning lecherously, she lightly stroked him. "Let me know if this tickles."

Now it was Fargo who arched his back and whose breath caught in his throat. The sensations she provoked sent waves of raw pleasure coursing through him. As he bent to kiss her, he thought he heard a sound but dismissed it as unlikely. The door was bolted, the windows were shut. He started to suck on her silken tongue.

The next moment, the sound was repeated.

Twisting and partially rising, Fargo glanced through the doorway. He wondered if it could be the Ovaro.

"Don't stop, handsome," Sarah said in a husky voice. "Whatever you do, please don't stop." Her fingers clamped onto his neck and she tried to pull him back down on top of her.

From the other room came an undeniable *thump*.

In a bound Fargo was off the bed, his back against the wall. Putting a finger to his mouth to warn Sarah not to say anything, he eased the Colt free.

Whoever was out there was in for a surprise.

5

Skye Fargo thumbed back the Colt's hammer and was poised to spring through the doorway when Sarah Arvin did the one thing he did not want her to do. She sat up and bawled loud enough to be heard in Salt Lake City, "Stop! What do you think you're doing?" The fear in her voice and on her face surprised him. They hadn't known one another long enough for her to care for him that much.

Crouching, Fargo swung past the jamb into the main room. Someone was trying to break into her home and had to be stopped. Taking three strides, he glanced around in bewilderment. The door and window were undisturbed, the curtains slack and motionless. Everything else in the room was as it should be.

Thinking that Sarah's shout had warned the intruder off, Fargo ran to the front door and threw the bolt. Shirtless, he rushed outside and on around the side. No one was there. Nor were there any footprints in the soil under the window. Fargo surveyed the woods and the creek, but the only sign of life was a fluttering yellow butterfly.

From inside Sarah called, "Skye? Where are you?"

Another possibility struck Fargo and he raced to the corral. But the poles in the gate were undisturbed, and the Ovaro hadn't moved since he saw it last.

Fargo was at a loss to account for the sounds he had heard. Lowering the Henry's hammer, he retraced his steps. Now he had two mysteries to solve. Floyd's disappearance, and this. For the moment, though, the bulge in his pants needed to be tended to.

Sarah was waiting in the middle of the main room. Her dress was down around her waist, and her hands were on her shapely hips. With her disheveled hair and pink flush to her face, she was the image of a ripe peach just begging to be bitten into. But she was also angry, and she lashed out with, "What in hell was that all about? Why would anyone in their right mind jump up and run off in the middle of making love?"

"I heard something," Fargo said while closing and bolting the door.

"I didn't hear anything. Are you sure that's all it was? Maybe I wasn't good enough for you," Sarah said archly. "Maybe you were bored."

Walking over, Fargo placed his hands on her shoulders. "Be serious."

"I am. It's been my experience that most women take making love much more serious than men do. I don't give myself to just anyone you know!"

Fargo thought she was making too much of a fuss, but he wisely didn't stoke her wrath by telling her. "I've never met a woman who excited me more," he stretched the truth a shade. "From the moment I set eyes on you, I couldn't wait to get you into bed."

"Oh?" Sarah brightened and switched her hands to his hips. "Then why are we standing here flapping our gums when we could be taking up where we left off?"

Once again Fargo scooped her into his arms, set her on the bed, and stretched out beside her. Removing his gunbelt, he placed the Colt within quick reach. His boots hit the floor. Seconds later the Arkansas toothpick joined the Colt.

Sarah squirmed with impatience, her fingers running languidly up and down her sides. "A girl could age ten years waiting on you," she groused.

"Your turn," Fargo said, and began stripping her bare. First, he finished removing her dress. Then he undid the stays to the pair of petticoats she wore and tossed the petticoats aside. She also wore a corset which she didn't need. As slim as she was about the waist, she had no need to reduce her waistline even more. But some women, like some men, were exceedingly vain.

Most corsets, like this one, had the fasteners at the front. He uncoupled them one by one, a time consuming task in itself, while she toyed with the hair at the nape of his neck and playfully rimmed his ear with a forefinger.

Finally, Fargo was down to her chemise and cotton drawers. "A man could age ten years undressing most women." He said, and untied the bow at the top of her chemise.

"It adds to the anticipation," was her rebuttal.

Fargo had long been amused by the female passion for clothes. Frontiersmen generally settled for owning a couple of shirts and pants. The same with most farmers and rural folks. Townsmen generally owned several sets. But there wasn't a man alive who could hold a candle to a woman when it came to their wardrobe. Dresses, skirts, blouses, corsets, chemises, stockings, shoes, hats, bonnets; the list went on and on. For every article a man wore, a woman had ten.

About a decade ago a woman by the name of Amelia Bloomer had tried to change all that. Newspapers everywhere carried stories about her and her peculiar trait of going around dressed much like a man. Instead of wearing dresses, she favored a loose-fitting, knee-length shirt and baggy ankle-length trousers that became known as bloomers. She claimed it was much more practical and vastly more comfortable. A few women followed suit but most laughed her to scorn, and the idea of women wearing pants had faded.

Personally, Fargo liked the notion. But not the baggy bloomers Amelia Bloomer wore. He'd like to see women in tight pants. The tighter, the better. So tight, every curve and contour could become a feast for the eye. Not that it would ever happen. But a gent could always dream.

A fingernail dug into Fargo's neck, ending his reverie.

"I swear! Are you going to lie there daydreaming all afternoon, or pay some attention to me?"

"I wore myself out undressing you," Fargo cracked, and was soundly punched on the shoulder. He could take a hint. Parting her chemise, he exposed her left breast. It was as full around as a cantaloupe and as supple as soft clay. Curving delightfully upward, the nipple was already as hard as a nail and as inviting as a succulent berry. Inhaling it, Fargo flicked the tip with his tongue.

"At last," Sarah moaned, and sculpted the hard muscles on his shoulders and upper arms.

Switching to her other breast, Fargo lathered it until it glistened. He cupped both mounds and squeezed. A low, urgent cry of craving escaped Sarah, and she rubbed her right leg against his pole. He kept on fondling and squeezing and pinching her breasts until her hips were rising and lowering of their own accord and she was mewing like a kitten.

"More! I want more, handsome!"

So did Fargo. He smothered her sultry lips with his own, as his left hand dipped down to her cotton drawers. Within moments he had them around her knees. At the contact of his hand on her inner thigh, Sarah exhaled as loudly as a blacksmith's bellows and pulled him closer. Her skin was exquisitely smooth. He ran his finger up and down and around and around but refrained from touching her core to heighten her suspense.

Patience wasn't Sarah's strong suit. "What are you waiting for? A written invitation?"

Gluing his mouth to her neck, Fargo suddenly swooped his hand to her moist crevice. Sarah groaned and dug her nails into his skin deep enough to draw drops of blood. Ignoring the pain, he inserted a finger between her nether lips and delicately slid it up and down.

Pulling back, Sarah purred huskily, *"Yesssss! Yesssss!* Just like that!"

Fargo's finger brushed her swollen knob, and she came up off the bed as if jolted by a bolt of lightning. Her fiery mouth was everywhere, kissing and licking, nibbling his face, his ears, his throat, his shoulders. Stiffening his forefinger, he lanced it up into her.

Sarah threw back her head, her mouth agape in a soundless scream of undiluted pleasure. Inserting a second finger, Fargo commenced to stroke in and almost out. Her legs parted to grant him greater access and he promptly eased between them. He felt her knees hook around his waist and her ankles lock at the small of his back.

"I want it! I want it so much!" Sarah whispered.

"It," Fargo noticed, not him. Moving his fingers faster, he soon had her panting as if she had run a mile. He glided his other hand through her soft hair and down her side to her breasts. Grasping a nipple between his thumb and finger, he pinched her—hard—while simultaneously driving the fingers of his other hand up into her with enough force to nearly lift her off the quilt.

"*Ahhhhhhhhhhh!* Do me, Skye! Please do me!"

Fargo's manhood was throbbing. Undoing his pants, he released it, and immediately Sarah's questing fingers wrapped tight. It brought a lump to his throat. When she pumped her arm, it was all he could do not to explode. Gritting his teeth, he flicked his thumb across her swollen knob and she trembled in lustful release.

"I can't hold off much longer, lover."

That was fine by Fargo. To send her over the brink, he inserted a third finger. A half-dozen strokes were enough. Sarah cried out and gushed, her inner walls rippling and contracting. Just at that moment, Fargo heard a slight sound from the other room. Raising his head, he listened but it wasn't repeated. His instinct was to investigate, but he had already angered Sarah once. If he were to jump out of bed now, she would be fit to be tied. Lowering his face to her flat stomach, he stuck his tongue into her belly button.

"You have no idea what you're doing to me!" Sarah exclaimed.

Fargo had a lot more in store. Rising onto his knees, he teased the end of his manhood along her drenched opening, causing her legs to quiver. Lust lighting her eyes, she gripped his hips and tried to impale herself on him but he pulled back, postponing their coupling.

"I want you in me!" Sarah demanded. "I want you in me right this second!"

Applying his mouth to her right breast, Fargo milked the other like he would a teat, pinching the nipple each time he came to the tip. She wriggled under him, her bottom churning against his iron member.

"Please! Oh, please!"

Rising onto his hands and knees, Fargo aligned his pulsing sword with her drenched sheath, tensed his legs, and rammed up into her. For a second or two it was as if Sarah was carved from stone. Then her eyes widened and she heaved her whole body up off the quilt as if in a bid to toss him off. Sinking back, she wrapped her legs around him tightly and unleashed a frenzy of lustful ardor that surpassed his own. All Fargo had to do was hold on and relish the ride. She bucked. She thrashed. She spurted—not once, but twice.

Then, like Old Faithful bursting from the earth, Fargo's own release occurred. His manhood exploded. The room blurred and danced. Closing his eyes, he rode the crest of an internal wave of pure bliss. When it subsided, as it always inevitably did, he drifted on a tranquil inner sea. His body slowed and his heartbeat returned to normal. Caked with sweat, he rolled off of Sarah and lay on his back, a forearm across his forehead.

"You were marvelous, lover," Sarah praised him between deep breaths. "Simply marvelous."

Their lovemaking had taken more out of Fargo than usual. He was so tired he couldn't stay awake. Deep, dreamless sleep claimed him, sleep his worn body wouldn't be denied. When in due course he opened his eyes, he lay in near total darkness. The bedroom door was shut, the room as quiet as a tomb.

Groping the bed, Fargo discovered he was alone. Sarah must be in the other room, maybe cooking their supper. He sat up, stretched, and slid off. In no great hurry, he donned his buckskins, strapped the toothpick around his ankle, and tugged his boots on. Lastly, he strapped on his gunbelt.

The nap had done him wonders. Fargo felt more refreshed than he had in days. He was also famished. Opening the door, he took a step, but only one. Something was amiss. The rest of the cabin was as dark as the bedroom. No lamps had been lit. No fire glowed in the hearth. And most perplexing of all, Sarah was gone.

Moving to the window, Fargo cracked the burlap curtains. Stars dominated the sky. By the position of the North Star, it was pushing pushing ten o'clock. Much too late for Sarah to be out and about.

His hand on the Colt's smooth grips, Fargo went to the front door and lifted the latch. Nothing happened. The door refused to open. The reason was literally in front of his nose; the bolt hadn't been thrown. Sarah couldn't possibly be outside, not unless she went out through a window.

Stumped, Fargo walked to the table. In the center was a lamp. He was lifting the glass globe when a faint glow, down low, caught his eye. Belatedly, he realized the chair Sarah had placed on top of the rug had been moved, and the rug itself rolled up and pushed under the chair. The glow came from a pale light rimming the trapdoor to the root cellar.

Squatting, Fargo gripped the rope handle and cautiously hiked the door high enough to peek down inside. A lantern hung from a peg on a post near the ladder. On shelves that lined three of the walls were slabs of jerked venison, potatoes, roots, acorns, and more. The fourth wall was in shadow.

"Sarah?" Fargo whispered. He couldn't say why he felt the need for caution—unless it was the rash of tiny pinpricks crawling across his skin. Bracing a boot on the second rung, he dipped down low enough to scan the entire cellar. A few tools were in one corner. In another, clothes were piled in a heap.

Then Fargo saw the fourth wall clearly. Or, rather, the lack of one. For there, framed by sturdy timbers, was a tunnel that branched off into the bowels of the earth. Descending to the bottom, he helped himself to the lantern and held it aloft. He drew the Colt and ventured a few yards into the dank shaft. He wasn't a miner, but he recognized a relatively recent excavation when he saw one. The timbers were new, and there wasn't much dust, or even a single spider web.

It had to be part of the Dirt Breathers' network of tunnels. But why did it come out under Sarah Arvin's cabin? Granted, she hated Vrittan, but that wouldn't account for the Dirt Breathers going to all the trouble of linking a shaft to her homestead.

Fargo had only himself to blame for not suspecting sooner that there must be another way out of the cellar. He remembered Sarah's comment about Clarence when he asked if the mute had left while they were outside: "Yes, but not how you think."

Extending the lantern in front of him, Fargo explored deeper. The tunnel bore straight for over a hundred yards, to a junction. There, two branches angled off into the darkness, both braced by ancient timbers buttressed by recent crossbeams. Part of the original mine, Fargo guessed, reinforced by the Dirt Breathers. He peered down one branch and then the other. Which to take? Hunkering, he examined the tunnel floor.

Sarah's cabin must be popular. Dozens of overlapping footprints indicated frequent visitors. Among them were Clarence's distinct oval tracks. Since most of the prints lead into or came out of the right branch, Fargo bent his steps the same way.

Dust covered the timbers, the walls, the ceiling. It was an inch thick on the ground. Tiny puffs rose with every step Fargo took. He didn't like how some of the old beams creaked and groaned, and he tried not to dwell on the outcome should the tons of dirt and rock above him come crashing down.

Fargo counted each step to give himself some idea of how far he went. Approximately two hundred yards from the first junction he came to another. This time there were three branches to chose from. Two were so overrun by footprints choosing between them could be impossible. Sliding a coin from a pocket, Fargo flipped it into the air. Heads would be to the right, tails to the left.

The coin landed tails up.

His back to a wall, Fargo hiked on. He hoped to find Sarah, or barring that, to meet some of the so-called Dirt Breathers and learn more about their dispute with Charlie Vrittan and the Air Breathers.

The tunnels went on forever. Twice more Fargo came to junctions, and each time he took the branch that had seen the most foot traffic. Of the Dirt Breathers there was no sign. He was beginning to think he had the tunnels all to himself when, on rounding a bend, he beheld a pair of shadowy shapes up ahead. They stood a short distance beyond the ring of lantern light, as if they had been waiting for him. He couldn't tell much about them other than they were both big and pale and might be wearing hides, like Clarence.

Halting, Fargo waited for them to say something. When neither did, he smiled and called out, "I'm a friend of Sarah Arvin's. Can you tell me where to find her?"

The ghostly apparitions didn't respond.

"I mean you no harm." To stress the fact, Fargo shoved the Colt into its holster. "I'd be obliged for your help."

Both figures began to slowly back away.

"Wait!" Fargo said. "Don't you know Sarah? The woman who lives in a cabin north of town? She told me she's a friend of yours." He took a step.

Pivoting, the pair sped back down the tunnel as if in fear for their lives.

Fargo swore under his breath and gave chase, but hadn't gone twenty yards when the lantern flickered and nearly died. It would be just his luck to use up the kerosene when he needed it most. Since he couldn't very well turn back, he held to a steady jog until another junction appeared. The lantern faded and brightened a second time. At any moment it might go out.

This time it was the right branch that saw the most use. Fargo headed into it, then heard a noise from the other tunnel. Spinning, he caught sight of the two Dirt Breathers as they whirled and fled. "Wait, damn it!" he hollered, but they showed no inclination to stop.

Fargo ran after them. The light the lantern cast faded to a feeble glow and stayed that way. It lent the illusion that the walls were closing in, and that the shadows were threatening to engulf him. Shrugging the feeling off, Fargo continued on to yet another junction, and stopped. The timbers here were laced with scores of cracks. They hadn't been buttressed and it wouldn't take much to bring them crashing down.

Twin tunnels forked at sharp angles, tunnels inches deep in dust. From them came a strange odor, like rotten fruit.

Some of the original Spanish diggings, Fargo figured, long abandoned. Two sets of fresh footprints led into the left fork. He opened his mouth to call out, to try and get it through their thick skulls he wasn't out to hurt them. But a glance at the sagging timbers gave him second thoughts.

Turning, Fargo considered going back. There were only one problem. There had been so many junctions, so many turns and bends, it would take him a year to find his way back to the root cellar. For one of the few times in his life, he was lost. Completely, hopelessly lost.

Without the sun and the stars to guide him, Fargo had to rely on his inner sense of direction. On cloudy and rainy days above ground that was enough. But down here it was different. He had absolutely no idea which way was north, south, east or west. And as if that were not bad enough, the glow from the lantern now barely reached his feet.

Fargo needed the Dirt Breathers' help. He entered the left tunnel, proceeding slowly. The smell grew stronger, the air noticeably cooler. He was deep underground, as deep as he had ever been, deeper than he had ever hankered to go. A miner's life wasn't for him. The confined space, the lack of fresh air, the possibility of being entombed alive, spiked him with unease. Men who made their living boring through the earth, daily toiling great depths below the surface, deserved his highest respect. Give him the wide-open prairies and the sweeping grandeur of majestic mountains any day.

The lantern abruptly died. Fargo shook it to confirm that the kerosene was gone. Since it was no longer of any use, he let it drop and wished he hadn't when the glass globe shattered loud enough to be heard from a considerable distance.

Holding his hands out in front of him, Fargo groped his way deeper into the tunnel. He counted his steps and was at thirty-seven when a sound stopped him cold. It was the sound of heavy breathing. Someone was only a few yards in front of him. "Who's there?" he asked, dropping his hand to his Colt. "Is it you two again?"

They didn't reply.

"I'm a friend of Sarah Arvin's," Fargo reiterated. "Do you know her?"

More breathing, but that was all.

Fargo was about at the end of his patience. "Answer me, damn you! I'm an outsider but I'd like to help you in your fight with Vrittan. Take me to Sarah. Or to your leader." He paused to let them respond, but they were as tight-lipped as ever. "What the hell is the matter with you?"

The heavy breathing receded. They were moving away.

"Wait! You know these tunnels. I don't." Fargo hurried to catch them, his left arm extended to keep from bumping into a wall. The air became colder yet, and was laced with the scent of moisture. "Hold up, you stupid sons of—"

Fargo's left boot swung into emptiness. He tried to throw himself backward but the dirt under his right boot gave way. Flailing wildly, he sought to check his fall and couldn't. He dropped like a stone, some fifteen to twenty feet. Although he kept his legs under him, he was thrown off balance when he hit, and stumbled to his knees. His right shoulder struck a wall with bone-jarring force.

Dazed, Fargo held himself still as sadistic laughter filtered from above. Then footsteps rapidly receded. The pair had lured him there on purpose and were leaving. But where was "there?" Gingerly, he felt about him and soon established he was in a pit roughly ten feet across.

Standing, he reached up as far as he could, straining on the tips of his toes, but couldn't reach the rim.

"Bastards," Fargo fumed. Putting his back against the wall, he paced toward the opposite side. It took three and a half steps. Again placing his back to the wall, he girded himself, took three quick strides, and leaped upward. His outstretched fingers smacked against the side of the pit, not the rim as he had hoped, and he fell back down.

Fargo wished he could get his hands on the two Dirt Breathers who had led him down there. It was highly probable they had left him there to rot. Without food and water he wouldn't last more than several days. But he would be damned if he would give up.

Fargo made another circuit, running his hand along the wall. There were no breaks, no gaps, no means of climbing out. Fair enough. He would make his own. Sinking onto his knee, he unstrapped the Arkansas toothpick. Soon he had several vertical niches dug, spaced a foot and a half apart, ideal for handholds and footholds. Jamming the toe of one boot into the lowest, he levered upward, then jammed the toe of his other boot into the next.

And so it went. By digging higher and higher niches, Fargo painstakingly worked his way toward the top. Dirt sifted into his hair and into his eyes, making them sting when he blinked. It wasn't as bad as the sand, but he had to constantly wipe them on his sleeves.

Along about the tenth or eleventh niche, Fargo reached up to dig another and his arm hooked the rim. He had done it! Raising both hands overhead, he pulled himself high enough to prop his elbows on the tunnel floor. In moments he was out of the pit and, after sheathing the toothpick, he rose and made off up the tunnel the way he had come.

Fargo walked as fast as he dared without risk of harming himself. It was important he conserve his energy. There was no telling how long it would take to reach the surface—if he ever did.

At the first few junctions it was easy to recollect which branch to take, but after that Fargo had to guess. He didn't own a pocket watch, so he couldn't say how much time elapsed. But it had to have been an hour or more when he heard a shuffling noise to his rear followed by guttural grunts.

The Dirt Breathers were hard on his heels.

Fargo had no inkling of how they had found him in that pitch-black soup. Maybe the decade they had spent underground lent them the ability to see in the dark, like cats. Or maybe their hearing was sharper. Whatever the case, they knew right where he was, and when he began to run, so did they.

It as an awful feeling, racing blindly down a tunnel that might end at any moment or turn in any direction. Fargo knew he could well crack his head on a timber or break a bone, leaving him at the mercy of his pursuers. Better, he thought, to make a stand. To find someplace where they couldn't rush him, and go down fighting.

Fargo's opportunity came sooner than he expected. Both hands in front of him, he blundered into the right-hand wall. Groping along, he established the tunnel curved ahead. And it occurred to him that if he waited just past the bend, the Dirt Breathers would be on top of him before they realized he was there. On top of him, and his blazing Colt. Hastening around the the bend, he wheeled.

It sounded like a herd of buffalo were after him.

Fargo leveled the Colt. Another couple of seconds and all hell would break loose.

Then huge arms corded with steely muscle coiled around him from behind.

6

Few men could manhandle Skye Fargo as if he were a
helpless child. He was a big man in his own right. Taller,
broader of shoulder, and stronger than most, he had
licked twice his weight in barroom drunks and saloon
toughs. So when the Colt was torn from his grasp with
ridiculous ease and he was unceremoniously upended
like a sack of potatoes and draped over a shoulder wider
than his own, he had a fair inkling who was responsible.
"Clarence? Is it you?"

His captor acknowledged the question with a grunt
that sparked a chorus of answering grunts from around
the bend.

Fargo wondered why the Dirt Breathers were doing
that all the time. Was it a way of communicating? "Clarence, you can let got of me."

Instead, the giant firmed his hold and trudged off up
the tunnel

Fargo debated whether to resist and decided against
it. Clarence was making no attempt to harm him. Or to
bind him.

Five or six pale spectral silhouettes tromped along in
their wake. The foremost was a stocky man who, judging
by the reek he gave off, hadn't taken a bath in a
coon's age.

Through gloomy tunnels without seeming end Fargo
was carried with as little effort as he would carry a leaf.
Clarence had the constitution of an ox, and never
flagged. At last they came to a fork and the tunnel floor
gradually sloped upward. Twisting, Fargo felt a breeze

on his face. Presently, they stepped from a mine entrance into a clearing ringed by tall firs and large boulders. Above them glittered a spectacular canopy of stars.

"Good work, Clarence." From out of the shadows materialized a willowy figure. "Put him down now."

Fargo was abruptly dumped onto his backside. Above him towered the deformed mute, who dropped the Colt between his legs.

"You're fortunate to be alive, handsome." Sarah Arvin said. "It's a good thing Clarence got to you before you were snared in one of the booby-traps down there."

Standing, Fargo brushed dirt off his leggings. "I fell into a pit. Does that count?"

Sarah took a quick stride and cupped his jaw. "Were you hurt? No broken bones or sprains, I hope?"

"I'm fine."

"Thank God! We can't afford to lose you. You're our ace in the hole. The key to our getting out of here alive. Or, to be more precise, your horse is." Sarah bit her lower lip. "I know how much that stallion means to you. Which makes this all the harder."

"Makes what?" Fargo asked, worried by her tone. His fatigue, and the dust caking his face and clothes, were forgotten.

"Sometime early tonight, while I was busy organizing the search for you, Charlie Vrittan's people stole the Ovaro from my corral."

Red-hot anger pumped through Fargo's veins. "Do you know where they took him?"

"In town, would be my guess. I sent a few Dirt Breathers to snoop around but they haven't gotten back to me yet." Sarah crooked a finger and headed through the boulders. "They have to be mighty careful. The Air Breathers shoot on sight."

The mine entrance was perched high on a mountainside on a bench that overlooked a winding valley. Sarah stood at the top of an incline and pointed at a smattering of lights thousands of feet below. "The town's not much to speak of. A dozen buildings, or thereabouts, some only half built. Vrittan holes up in what was to be the hotel. Down the street from it is a stable. That's where I think you'll find your pinto."

Clarence and another Dirt Breather Fargo had never seen before appeared out of nowhere.

"Did you fetch it like I told you?" Sarah asked the second man.

Grunting, the Dirt breather held out the Henry.

Fargo took it and levered a round into the chamber. "This is twice I'm in your debt," he told Arvin. "If there's ever anything I can do to repay you, all you have to do is say the word."

Sarah smiled thinly. "I'd never come right out and ask, but if you were to make buzzard bait of Charlie Vrittan, I'd consider our account settled."

Fargo wasn't a killer by nature, but he had no objections to putting a slug into Vrittan if the man tried to stop him from recovering the Ovaro. "I'm going after my horse. Wait for me at your cabin. If all goes well, I should show up sometime late tomorrow morning. If it doesn't—" He shrugged and started over the crest.

"Skye?" Sarah said, snagging his sleeve. "Be careful, you hear? I've grown sort of fond of you." She caressed his cheek. "I'd like to see you again."

"Be looking for me." Fargo set out, moving briskly. At that altitude the air was crisp and invigorating. He soon reached the bottom of the bench and entered a stand of spruce. He was well into it, moving as stealthily as a Sioux warrior, when he happened to glance over his shoulder and spied a bearish bulk slinking silently after him twenty yards back. Only one person in those parts was that big; Clarence.

It must be Sarah's doing, Fargo reasoned. She had sent the giant to keep an eye on him. To protect him. The woman was always thinking of others, always putting their welfare before her own. A rare trait. If he were the marrying kind, he could do a lot worse than Sarah Arvin.

Fargo pretended he wasn't aware Clarence was shadowing him. The next belt of trees consisted of a mix of deciduous and evergreens. Passing through them, it wasn't long before he heard the gurgle of swiftly flowing water and came out of the undergrowth on the bank of a creek. He had a hunch it was the same waterway that flowed past Sarah's place, well to the north.

Kneeling, Fargo dipped his head under the surface. It was like submersing himself in liquid ice. The cold eliminated every last tendril of lingering weariness. Pulling back, he shook his head to shed the excess water, then drank enough to quench his thirst.

The soft tread of stealthy steps brought Fargo around with the Henry wedged to his side, but it was only Clarence. Partially shrouded by the limbs of a pine, he gave the illusion of being carved from stone. "Were you sent to watch my back and make sure I make it out alive?" Fargo asked. He didn't really expect a reply.

Clarence pointed a finger as thick as a chisel at the town still a thousand feet below.

"In a hurry, are you?" Fargo said. Rising, he vaulted the creek and soon came to a grassy switchback that afforded a sweeping vista of the entire valley. Mountains hemmed it on all sides. High stone ramparts that effectively isolated it from the outside world. No wonder no one had paid it a visit since '49.

The grass swished, and Fargo was prodded in the back. Clarence was right behind him, pointing.

"I know where I'm going," Fargo said testily. He couldn't understand why the giant was being so insistent. He would reach the town soon enough.

Again Clarence jabbed him. Only then did Fargo sense the hostility the mute radiated. Something had Clarence extremely upset. So much so, Clarence clenched a gigantic fist and shook it in his face.

"What the hell has gotten into you?" Fargo held his ground.

A snarl escaped the man-brute's contorted lips. He touched a finger to his own chest, then swivelled and jabbed it up the mountain in the direction of the mine.

"Are you mad at Sarah for sending you to help me?"

Clarence suddenly seized Fargo by the front of the shirt and shook the same ponderous fist under his nose.

In sheer reflex, Fargo balled his own fist to strike, but didn't. A startling detail mesmerized him.

Glistening in the starlight, a tear was trickling from Clarence's left eye. It rolled down the mute's twisted cheek and over his lopsided mouth.

"You're crying?" Fargo said in astonishment. "Why, Clarence? What's the matter?"

The giant whined, then let go and took a step back, tossing his great head from side to side. More tears flowed, and he uttered a low sob.

"Clarence?" Fargo said. He was thoroughly baffled. After all the poor misfit had done in his behalf, he would like to help. It was Clarence, after all, who took the Ovaro to Sarah so she could doctor it. Clarence who had brought him safely out of the mine. Fargo had grown to like the stripling. "I thought we were friends. Are you mad at me?"

A louder sob rose to the stars. Wheeling, Clarence bolted up the mountain as if a horde of Comanches were nipping at his heels. The forest soon swallowed him. Moments later, from out of its depths came a soul-seared wail.

"What the hell?" Fargo said softly. The mute's behavior made no sense. What had Clarence been trying to tell him? It gave him a lot to ponder as he continued down the mountain until he was crouched in timber a hundred yards above the town of Vrittan.

Calling it a town, though, was being charitable. The plank buildings were in severe disrepair. Some had never even been finished. Doors hung from only one hinge or were missing altogether. None of the windows contained glass panes. The few hitchrails were broken, weeds littered the single street. And everywhere there was dust; caking the walls, the roofs, the plank boardwalk. It was a ghost town waiting to happen.

The stable was at the near end. Twice the size of the other structures, it had wide double doors, both of which were shut, and no windows that Fargo could see. In a crouch, sticking to the shadows, he crept on around to the front.

The town was as quiet as a cemetery. Lights blazed from three different buildings clustered close together further down.

Fargo crept to the center of the wide doors. They weren't barred from within. Sliding his fingers between them, he slowly pulled the right-hand door open. Although he only opened it wide enough to slip inside, its long-neglected hinges creaked much too loudly. No sounds or movements greeted his entry. The air was musty and smelled of dust and old wood, not straw and hay and horse droppings as a stable should. After giving his eyes a few seconds to adjust to the near-total darkness, Fargo glided toward a row of stalls. He went from one to the other until he came to the rear. They were empty. And from the look of things, none had been used in years.

Fargo was at a loss. Where else would Charlie Vrittan keep the Ovaro? Was it tied behind one of the other buildings where it was less likely to be found? He started toward the wide doors, then froze.

Someone had just slipped inside.

Hunkering, Fargo watched an indistinct figure warily approach the stalls. He heard a gun hammer click. Careful not to make a sound, he slid into the last stall and squatted with his back to the inner wall. He quietly set the Henry down, reached under his pant leg, and palmed the Arkansas toothpick.

A shoe scraped the ground awfully near.

Fargo held his breath, and tensed. It must be a guard. The Air Breathers would naturally be on constant guard against a Dirt Breather attack. Either the man had spotted him entering the stable, or had seen the open door and decided to investigate. Another second, and the dark figure came abreast of the stall opening.

Fargo could tell the man was slight of build and not all that tall. Not all that sharp-eyed, either, because the man didn't spot him, and turned toward the hayloft. Uncoiling, Fargo launched himself at the Air Breather's back. The impact bowled the guard over. As they sprawled to the hard-packed dirt floor, Fargo wrapped his left arm around the fellow's thin frame while simultaneously gouging the tip of the toothpick into the man's neck and warning, "Not a peep or I'll slit you from ear to ear!"

The guard stiffened but didn't cry out. His hat had fallen off, and a mane of hair spilled across Fargo's chest. At the same instant, Fargo realized his left arm wasn't clamped onto lean muscle but on twin mounds the size of large apples. The scent of lavender enveloped him. Shocked, he lowered the toothpick and blurted, "You're a woman!"

"And you're no Dirt Breather," was her calm reply. "Is it you, Jimmy? I told you before you're not my type. If Charlie hears of this he'll have you skinned alive."

She mistook him for another Air Breather, Fargo realized. "I'm from the outside," he whispered. "I'm here after my horse."

"The outsider!"

Fargo felt her whole body go as rigid as a branding iron. She tried to wriggle loose, but he refused to let her up just yet. Woman or not, she was one of Vrittan's underlings, and that made her a potential enemy.

"You're him, aren't you? The one Moran and Bokor told us about? The one who was at the Black Widow's place?"

"Who?" Fargo found himself distracted by the fragrance of her hair and the firm contours of her pert bottom against his groin.

"That bitch, Sarah Arvin. We call her the Black Widow, after the spider. She's just as deadly and ten times as diabolical." The woman paused. "Please. Let me up. I won't try anything. I promise."

"See that you don't." Slowly rising, Fargo unwrapped his arm from around her breasts. To keep her from running off, he clamped his hand onto her shoulder, then said, "All I want is my pinto. What have your people done with him?"

"Is this some kind of trick?" she responded. "You know darn well your horse is at the Black Widow's."

Fargo was glad it was dark so his confusion wouldn't

show. She sounded sincere, but she had to be lying. "Sarah told me your people stole him. I came to get him back."

"You can search the whole town but you won't find him," the Air Breather said indignantly. "I'd stake my life that the Black Widow took him. She doesn't want anyone to leave these mountains until she's good and ready, and she'll go to any lengths to stop them." The woman offered her hand. "I'm Olivia Dixon, by the way. Who might you be?"

Fargo told her.

"I'm pleased to make your acquaintance. You're the first outsider to make it this far. The last one was dragged into the tunnels before we had a chance to warn him what was in store."

"Sarah Arvin said I was the first outsider she's seen since she came here."

"Ah. Well, the Black Widow wouldn't know the truth if it jumped up and bit her. She's evil, mister, through and through. Because of her a lot of good people have died. Because of her, a lot of other good people, like me, have been trapped in these god-awful mountains for years." Olivia's voice became laced with anger. "Over a decade of my life has been lost! A decade never recover! I hate her, mister. I hate her, mister. I hate her more than words can say."

Fargo recollected that Sarah Arvin had said basically the same thing about Charlie Vrittan. One or the other had to be lying, and he was determined to learn which. "We need to talk, but not here." Not when her friends might show up at any moment. "Is there somewhere we can go where we won't be disturbed?"

"There's my room. I have it all to myself. And there are some things there I'd like to show you. Things that will expose the Black Widow for the wicked creature she is."

"Fair enough. But first—" Fargo pulled Dixon toward the last stall.

Digging in her heels, the woman grabbed his wrist and

demanded, "What are you up to? Try having your way with me, and so help me, I'll scratch your eyes out!"

"Don't get your hopes up, lady," Fargo said dryly. "All I want is my rifle."

"Oh."

Fargo had her walk in front of him to the wide doors, the Henry's muzzle against her spine. "Hold up," he directed, and scanned the street. No one else was out and about, which was suspicious in itself. "It's still early yet. Where is everyone?"

"Inside, where it's safer. The Dirt Breathers come out at night, and they can see in the dark a lot better than we can."

"What were you doing outside, then?"

"Sentry duty. We take turns. Even the women. As Charlie says, we all have to pull our own weight."

Fargo supposed she was on the level. "Where's your room?"

"In the fourth building down, on the right."

Near ones that were lit up, Fargo noticed. It could be a trap, and Olivia Dixon could be the bait being used to lure him in. "We'll go around the back way," he directed. "Don't call out. And no sudden movements."

"Or what? You'll blow a hole in me?" Olivia chuckled. "Somehow you don't impress me as being a cold-blooded murderer. You're not like the Black Widow."

"Get walking."

Sudden laughter came from the two-story building farther down. A silhouette was framed in a lit window, but only for a few seconds.

Olivia Dixon moved like a doe being stalked by wolves. Stepping as lightly as if she were walking on egg shells, she peered intently off into the nearby woods. When a twig snapped, she sucked in an anxious breath and turned to stone.

"I'm alone," Fargo whispered to put her at ease.

"You only think you are," was her reply. "The Dirt Breathers are always out there at night, lurking, waiting for a chance to pick one of us off. The only reason they haven't wiped us out is because they ran out of ammunition long ago. We were smarter. We used ours sparingly."

"Keep going," Fargo said, giving her a nudge. "And don't worry. I won't let anyone harm you."

Olivia walked faster. Darting from the rear of one building to the next, she soon came to the one where she lived. There was a back door but it had long since been boarded up. The same with a rear window. Gesturing, she guided him around to the front.

"Stop," Fargo commanded when they came to the corner. Again he scanned the street from south to north and back again. Muffled voices came from nearby dwellings, among them that of a small girl reciting a nursery rhyme. "How many children are here?"

"Eleven young ones," Olivia answered. "We do the best we can, but we're handicapped by being cut off from the rest of the world. The poor kids have no real notion of what they're missing."

Fargo touched her shoulder and she hurried to the front door. He glued himself to her side and was taken aback when she halted to fish for a key in her pocket. They were in plain sight. Anyone looking out an adjacent window would spot them. Whipping the Henry to his shoulder, he whispered, "Hurry it up!"

"Relax, mister. No one here will lift a finger against you." Olivia inserted the key, and twisted. "Whether you know it or not, you're our salvation."

Following her in, Fargo had only taken a couple of steps when the nasal rasp of loud snoring fell on his ears. Grabbing Dixon, he pushed her against the wall. "What are you trying to pull?" he whispered. "I thought you claimed you had this place all to yourself?"

Unruffled, Olivia responded, "My room, yes, but not the entire house. Four other people live here. Two men downstairs and another woman upstairs."

Fargo didn't like it. He didn't like it one little bit. "Are they all asleep?"

"Just old Bill. He's getting on in years and always turns in early. The others are down the street at the

74

hotel. Most everyone gathers there in the evening for socializing and such." She placed her hand on his. "Trust me. I would never mislead you."

"Trust you? Hell, I only just met you." Fargo didn't know what to make of it when she grinned as if he had told a joke.

Holding onto his hand, Olivia turned onto a flight of stairs. At the second floor landing she bobbed her chin at a door on the left. "That's my friend's room. Maggie. She lost her husband to the Dirt Breathers."

The door on the right was locked. Again Olivia fished for a key, and once they were inside, she shooed him to one side and slid a large wooden bar into a pair of evenly spaced brackets on the back of the door. "From time to time the Dirt Breathers break into our buildings in the middle of the night," she explained. "A close friend of mine was taken from her very bed not two months ago. I'll be damned if the same will happen to me."

Her furniture consisted of a chest of drawers, a small table, a bed, and a single chair. Fargo moved to the window, which was covered by a pink sheet, and was about to peer out when suddenly a match flared behind him. Springing back, he trained the Henry on her. "Are you trying to get me caught?"

"We need light to see, don't we?" Olivia tapped a lamp in the center of the table. "With your permission?"

"Go ahead," Fargo said gruffly. So long as he avoided the window he should be safe enough. She bent low, and the next moment a soft rosy glow bathed the room. Puffing on the match, she turned.

For the first time Fargo saw her clearly—and he liked what he saw. She had luxuriant brunette hair that framed an oval face. Deep-blue eyes, full cheeks, and lips shaped into a perpetual delectable pout completed her portrait. She was petite but had an hourglass figure most women would die for. Her breasts, although not half as big as Sarah Arvin's, were nicely rounded. She wore a man's shirt and a man's pants, both altered to fit her smallish build. "Is there a shortage of dresses?" he bantered.

Olivia didn't bat an eye. "Yes, as a matter of fact,

there is. And a shortage of fabric and thread to sew new ones." She touched her flannel shirt. "These belonged to my brother, God rest his soul."

"What happened to him?"

"Need you ask? The Dirt Breathers. Four years ago, it was. A group of women went to wash clothes at the creek and were attacked. When Johnny rushed to help, he was killed by the big one. The Beast, we call him. Although his real name is Clarence." Almost as an afterthought, Olivia remarked, "He's the Black Widow's son."

Fargo's amazement must have shown.

"What? You don't believe me? Ask anyone here. They'll confirm it."

"Arvin said her son was named Maxwell. She said her husband and him went for help but never made it back."

Olivia indulged in brittle laughter. "She's fed you a whole passel of lies, hasn't she? Maxwell was a farmer from Kentucky, a good friend of Frank Arvin's. She had them both killed when they wouldn't join in her crusade to lay claim to all the gold."

"She murdered her own husband?" Fargo moved to the chair and slowly sat. Could it truly be that Sarah had deceived him? Or was Olivia Dixon manipulating him for her own ends? "In the stable you mentioned something about proof."

Nodding, Olivia walked to the chest of drawers. From it she took a folded sheet of paper. "This was found stuck to the front door the day after Johnny was killed. It speaks for itself."

Fargo unfolded it. The sheet had been torn from a child's school tablet, by the looks of it. The ink was faded, confirming the letter was indeed at least several years old. The letter read:

Dear Olivia, I was sorry to hear about your
brother, but he brought it on himself. When
will you and the rest come to your senses? When
will this senseless slaughter end? My way is the
right way and you know it. We were friends once.

*I would like to think we can be friends again.
Come over to our side, Olivia. Show the rest of
Vrittan's misguided supporters they're on the
losing side. I will greet you with open arms.*

It was signed "Sarah." He sat back and looked at
Dixon. "This doesn't tell me a thing."

"Didn't you read the part about the rest of us coming
to our senses? And how her way is the right way?"

"So? Your side thinks they're in the right. I don't see
any difference."

Olivia shook her head in disbelief. "She sure has
pulled the wool over your eyes. But I've got something
else here that—" She stopped, her head cocked to one
side.

Fargo heard it, too. From out in the street came a
babble of voices, and then the tramp of boots downstairs.
He pushed to his feet as the newcomers flowed up the
stairs and along the hall to Dixon's door. A fist pounded
several times.

"Olivia? We know you're in there! And we know the
outsider is with you! Open up or we'll kick the door in
and take him by force!"

7

Skye Fargo was cornered. Glaring at Olivia Dixon, he trained the Henry on the center of her door and snapped back the hammer. A few slugs should discourage the Air Breathers from trying to break it down, he reckoned.

"No! Don't!" Olivia cried, throwing herself in front of the rifle. "Please! Let me talk to them! You don't understand!"

Fargo understood, all right. And he was tired of being played for a jackass. Spinning, he darted to the window. More lamps had come on up and down the street, and Air Breathers were gathering in front of the hotel. But at the moment no one was directly below. Grabbing the chair in his left hand, he heaved it up off the floor.

"What are you doing?" Olivia exclaimed, cowering back and raising her arms to protect herself. "Hurting me won't accomplish anything!"

Fargo agreed. Blows rained on the door as he whirled and hurled the chair with all his might. It struck the pink sheet and exploded outward, ripping the makeshift curtain from the thin rod on which it hung, and sending it flapping out into the street. In a bound he was at the sill. Flinging his right leg over, he slid out, balanced for a moment on the edge of the sill, then dropped.

"No! Come back!" Olivia shouted. "I can set everything right!"

It was too late for that. Fargo dropped feet first, let his legs absorb the brunt of landing, and was up and off like a thoroughbred out of a starting gate. But he hadn't gone five yards when a pair of husky men came barreling out of the shadows to block his escape. One raised a hand for him to halt.

"Like hell," Fargo fumed, and drove the Henry's hard-wood stock into the Air Breather's gut. The second man clutched at his arm, but tearing loose, Fargo arced the stock into the man's temple.

Olivia was at her window. "Stop! I beg you! They only want to talk to you!"

Barely were the words out of her mouth when a rifle cracked near the hotel and a dirt geyser spewed next to Fargo's leg. Rotating, he snapped off three swift shots, aiming over their heads so as not to accidentally hit any women or children.

Pandemonium reigned. Men bellowed in anger, women screamed in panic. Above the uproar rose a voice that might have been that of Charlie Vrittan himself. "Stop him! We can't let him leave!"

Fargo veered into a benighted gap between the buildings and flew toward the forest. Air Breathers were in furious pursuit. As he came to the far end, darkling forms filled the street side. Slanting to the right to avoid being shot in the back, he hurtled into chest-high weeds and plowed through to the tree line.

Air Breathers streamed after him from around several points.

"There he is!" a woman yelled.

"After him!" a man urged.

It was tempting to drop a few, but instead Fargo plunged into the woods and soon outdistanced even the fleetest. He pressed on for another half of a mile, and finally paused to catch his breath on a slope midway to the old mine. Roosting on a log, he stared down at the lights of the town. Now he had two conflicting accounts to weigh, Arvin's and Dixon's. Only one of them could be telling the truth, but which one was it? Sarah had taken him in, nursed him, and tended the Ovaro. She was kind, considerate, and caring, hardly the wicked killer Olivia made her out to be. The letter Olivia claimed was proof of Sarah's wicked nature could just as well have been a sincere expression of regret concerning the death of Olivia's brother.

One thing was for sure. A great evil was loose amid these mountains. Spawned by greed, it had resulted in the deaths of many innocents and a nightmarish existence for those still alive. The Air Breathers and the Dirt Breathers had hated each other for so long, both sides were all too willing to believe the worst of the other, and proof be damned.

The bloodshed must end. The stranded emigrants must be brought out of the wilderness so they could get on with their lives. But it was more than one man could accomplish. The army was better suited to the task. And to reach the nearest fort, Fargo needed the Ovaro. It angered him to no end that the stallion had become a crucial pawn in the war between the two factions. There would be hell to pay if it came to any harm. Fargo would see that those responsible paid, and paid dearly.

Some might say it was strange for a man to become so attached to a horse. But when a man and an animal have been together as long as Fargo and the Ovaro, when they have endured hard times together and saved each other's skin on more occasions than Fargo cared to count, it didn't seem so strange, after all.

Not all horses were equal. No two were ever alike. There were dependable ones and not-so-dependable ones. There were horses that could be ridden from dawn until dusk and hardly ever tire, and others so lazy and contrary they weren't worth being saddled. Some had better dispositions than others. Those worth their salt would ride themselves into the ground if it were required of them. Others would bite a man the second his back was turned. The Ovaro possessed the best of all those traits, and was, quite simply, the finest horse Fargo had ever come across.

Yes, there would be hell to pay, indeed.

Suddenly Fargo sensed he was no longer alone. Leaping up, he brandished the Henry as five pale-skinned figures clothed in hide and tattered old clothes strode out of the shadows. Dirt Breathers, but Clarence wasn't among them. "What do you want?" Fargo asked.

A filthy man with a shock of red hair pointed up the mountain toward the mine.

"You want me to follow you up? Is that it?" Fargo guessed. "Why don't you just come right out and say so?"

The man didn't respond.

"Cat got your tongue?" Fargo snapped, and stalked toward him. He was sick and tired of the Dirt Breathers acting so high and mighty around him. Back in the tunnels, they hadn't answered him once. "I asked you a question. Talk, damn you."

Taking a step back, the man vigorously shook his head.

"What's your name? How did you know where to find me? Were you spying on me while I was in town?"

The man glanced at the others, as if for support, then placed a hand over his mouth as if to say he wouldn't speak, and that was final.

"Is that so?" Fargo said, and clipped the man across the jaw with the Henry. The redhead fell to his knees, clasping his chin and groaning, and rocked from side to side. "Feel like talking yet? I can do this all night if I have to."

Another Dirt Breather, a woman in deer hides, sprang toward them.

Training the Henry on her, Fargo warned, "I wouldn't, lady, were I you. I'm not in the best of moods. Suppose you answer my questions instead of your friend, here."

The woman wagged her hands and shook her head.

Pressing the Henry's muzzle to the man's forehead, Fargo declared, "One of you sure as hell better answer me, and do it quick."

Mewing like a kitten, the woman rushed up close. Fargo elevated his rifle but held his fire. She wasn't attacking him, or trying to wrest the Henry away. She was holding her mouth wide open and pointing inside. "What the hell?"

The man on his knees grabbed at the woman's arm but she swatted his hand away and kept pointing into her open mouth with the other while making those peculiar mewing sounds.

"You want me to look in your mouth?" Wary of a trick, Fargo bent lower. There wasn't a lot of light, but he could see most of her teeth and the bottom of her mouth. It took a few moments for what he was seeing to fully sink in, and when it did, dawning horror rippled through him.

The woman slowly closed her mouth, and smiled.

"It can't be!" Turning, Fargo gripped the redhead's lower jaw. "Open yours." The man balked and shook his head. Hiking the Henry as if it were a club, Fargo growled, "Conscious or unconscious makes no difference to me."

Hissing in defiance, the redhead reluctantly complied, bending his head so Fargo could see better. One glance was enough. Stepping back, Fargo lowered his rifle and looked at each of the Dirt Breathers in turn. "All of you?" he said in disbelief and horror. "You've all had your tongues cut out?"

Each one nodded.

"But *why*?" To Fargo it was the ultimate madness. "Did someone do this to you? The Air Breathers, maybe?"

The woman and a couple of others shook their heads, and the woman laughed as if to say the idea was preposterous.

His mind whirling with the implications, Fargo thought of Clarence. He had assumed the giant was an ordinary mute, but now the terrible truth was revealed. "You're saying you did this to yourselves? Deliberately?"

They all grinned and proudly nodded.

Fargo was dumfounded. The Dirt Breathers cut out their own tongues! It was insane. He couldn't think of a single reason for them to mutilate themselves so. Yet there had to be one. In every other respect they appeared normal enough. There was one person who could explain. One person who knew more than she had revealed. Shouldering the Henry, he marched into the pines without a word to the others.

Immersed in thoughts as dark as the night, Fargo climbed swiftly. He had only one last slope to climb when a massive shape materialized beside him and fell into shambling step alongside him. "I thought you were mad at me," Fargo commented, glancing up.

Clarence sadly bowed his great head.

"If that's your way of saying you're sorry, your apology is accepted," Fargo said. "I just found out about your tongue. Did you cut it out yourself, or was it done to you when you were little?"

Frowning, Clarence held a huge hand about as high off the ground as Fargo's waist.

"So the children had it done to them whether they wanted it done or not." Fargo suppressed a shiver. More Dirt Breathers sprouted out of the vegetation. By the time he came to the clearing in front of the mine, he was surrounded.

Sarah Arvin was there, seated on a boulder, impatiently tapping her fingers. Hearing them, she leaped up and grinned in joy. "Skye! You made it out safely!" She ran up, threw her arms wide, and embraced him. "I was so worried! We heard gunfire."

"They weren't very friendly," Fargo said.

"Did you run into Charlie Vrittan? If so, I hope you shot the bastard dead," Sarah commented hopefully.

"I never set eyes on the man."

"Damn." Disappointed, but trying not to show it, Sarah gripped his shoulders, leaned back, and scanned the clearing. "Where's your stallion? Don't tell me he's still down there?"

"They claimed they never had him."

Sighing, Sarah stepped to one side and gazed off down the mountain. "Liars, the whole bunch of them. They'll say or do anything if it suits their purpose. They have him, all right. They left enough sign a child could find."

"I'd like to visit your corral and examine the tracks for myself."

Sarah's forehead creased. "What? You don't believe me? After all I've done for you and that animal of yours?"

"Why didn't you admit Clarence is your son? Or tell me that the Dirt Breathers all had their tongues cut out?"

For a few seconds Sarah was motionless. Then she moved toward the boulder she had been roosting on and sat back down. "So that's it. Who have you been talking to?"

"Olivia Dixon told me about Clarence—" Fargo began.

A string of unladylike obscenities spewed from Sarah. Her lovely face was twisted in sheer hatred so potent it blazed from her eyes like burning coals and curled her lips into a bestial grimace. "That bitch! Once, we were the best of friends. But that all changed when the gold was found. She's opposed me ever since. She even had the gall to turn my own husband against me! To convince him it was best if he went for help!"

The transformation struck Fargo like a physical blow. He had taken Arvin for one of the kindest, most unselfish people he'd ever met. "You've been lying to me all along, haven't you, Sarah?" he softly asked.

Arvin recoiled, her hand to her throat, and blinked several times. Gradually a new look came over her, a smug, crafty expression underlined by a hint of latent cruelty. This was the real Sarah Arvin. This was her true self. And the reality was enough to make Fargo feel queasy. "Not all the time, no. If I'm guilty of anything, it's lying by omission. I didn't want to upset you."

"Or could it be you knew I wouldn't take your side if you told the whole truth?" Fargo rejoined.

"Truth is flexible, handsome. The truth I live by might not be the same truth you live by. But you're right. I needed you. So I held back."

"Needed me for what?" Fargo asked. But she only smiled, so he supplied the reason himself. "Those people down there never stole my stallion. It was another of your lies. You sent me down there hoping I would do what you haven't yet been able to. Dispose of Charlie Vrittan."

Sarah sighed. "It would have made my life so much

simpler. With him out of the way the others would eventually fall in line. That wily little fox is the only reason they've held out against me as long as they have."

"It's been him against you all along, hasn't it? What did you do? Try to steal his gold? Was that what started this whole business?"

"Tried?" Sarah said, and laughed merrily. "Hell, the gold is ours, and has been for years. Ever since we took control of the tunnels." She idly motioned at the somber ring of pale men and women. "They're all in it with me. Like me, they weren't willing to settle for the pittance Charlie offered. Like me, they wanted larger shares. And now they'll get them, once we end this and can leave."

"End it how?"

Sarah snickered. "Need you ask? We can't very well leave Charlie's bunch alive to inform the authorities. Once we've wiped the last of them out, we can safely return to civilization. We'll blame all the deaths on the Utes."

There it was, plain as could be. Fargo's inside shriveled at the thought of how he had been used and manipulated. "Why have the Dirt Breathers cut out their tongues?"

"What better way to ensure none of us can give our secret away?" Sarah leaned back, grinning. "Once the mine was ours, we dug out all the ore and hid it. Charlie and those other simpletons have no idea where it is. They've caught a few of us from time to time and tried to make us talk, but they can't." She cackled gleefully. "Pretty brilliant on my part, don't you think?"

Fargo looked at the pale wretches who ringed the clearing. Since the dawn of time people had been willing to murder, maim, and butcher to acquire vast wealth. But this was the first time he ever heard of people mutilating themselves. They had been willing to give up the power of speech for the rest of their lives, and for what? "How much will each of their shares be worth?"

"Oh, we figure about half a million, give or take." Sarah chortled. "Enough for us to live in luxury the rest of our lives."

"Why is it you never had your own tongue cut out?"

"One of us needed to be able to talk. To deal with Charlie, if nothing else. Since I'm in charge, who better?"

"Awful convenient," Fargo commented. That left one last question, one she had avoided. "You still haven't said why you didn't tell me Clarence is your son. Are you ashamed to admit it?"

Bristling like a riled porcupine, Sarah declared, "How dare you! I love my boy, heart and soul." Beckoning to Clarence, she rose. He shambled over, his chin sheepishly tucked to his massive chest, and she put an arm around him. "I grant you he's not easy on the eyes. When he was small, our lives were hell. Other children would run screaming at the sight of him, and other parents didn't want him on their property. So Frank and I decided to move West. To go where there weren't as many people. To where we could live like ordinary folks."

"But you gave up on that idea when you found the gold," Fargo remarked, and turned toward Clarence. "How did you feel about your mother killing your father?"

A howl of outrage tore from Sarah. Her fingernails hooked to claw and rip, she flew at him.

Fargo snapped the Henry to his shoulder, stopping her dead. "I've heard all I need to. You're going to lead me to the Ovaro or I'll start pumping lead into you, starting at the knees and working my way up."

"You wouldn't shoot a woman," Sarah scornfully snarled.

Working the lever, Fargo sighted on her left kneecap. "Not as a general rule, no. But in your case, lady, I'm more than willing to make an exception."

The Dirt Breathers had tensed and a few began to edge forward, but halted at a gesture from Arvin. "I believe you would at that. But what if I bleed to death? Or the wound becomes infected? What then? If I die, you'll never see your precious stallion again. I'm the only one who knows where it is."

Fargo scowled. She had him over a barrel and they both knew it.

Sarah slyly grinned and placed her hands on her hips. "I figured that would take some of the starch out of your bluster. Lower your rifle and I'll tell you how things are going to be."

An almost overwhelming urge to smash the Henry into her face came over him, but Fargo resisted it and let the muzzle dip a few inches.

"That's better but nowhere near good enough." Sarah held out a hand. "Give it to me. Then unbuckle your belt and shed the Colt. And let's not forget that nasty knife you carry under your boot."

"Go to hell."

"Bucking me could be an expensive proposition. I thought you gave a damn about whether your horse lives or dies. Or was I mistaken?"

"That works both ways. You need the Ovaro alive so when the time comes, someone can make it out and send back help. I'm calling your bluff."

Sarah chuckled and lowered her arm. "I reckon we have a standoff. For now you get to go your own way."

"Not alone," Fargo said. He had no intention of letting her out of his sight until he had recovered the pinto. "I'm taking you with me."

"Don't push your luck," Sarah chided. "Leave while you still can."

"It's not open to parley." Taking a quick step, Fargo grabbed her arm and moved toward the boulders. Two Dirt Breathers interposed themselves but backed off when he swung the Henry toward them.

"I can't let you do this," Sarah said.

"You can't stop me."

"No, but Clarence can."

Fargo spun, but her son was already in lightning swift motion. A hand with knuckles as big as walnuts wrapped around the Henry's barrel and it was wrenched from Fargo's grasp. He stabbed for the Colt but two other Dirt Breathers pounced. One tackled him about the waist, the other about the shins.

Slammed to the ground, Fargo fought to break loose. He punched one man in the jaw, the other in the ear.

The latter howled and let go, but by then more were piling on. A heavy Dirt Breather smashed onto Fargo's chest, a shoe clipped his skull. Still he resisted, landing solid blows right and left.

"Pin his arms, you simpletons!" Sarah Arvin shouted.

They tried. Fingers clamped onto Fargo's wrists and elbows, but he furiously tore free. A leering countenance filled his vision and he shattered its nose with an uppercut. Then a walking mountain blotted out the heavens and an iron hand closed on his throat and he was lifted high into the air and shaken as a grizzly might shake a marmot.

"That's my boy," Sarah proudly crowed.

Fargo was relieved of the Colt and the toothpick. Clarence set him down, but didn't remove the hand around the neck. Their eyes met, and Fargo swore he saw regret mixed with sorrow mirrored in Clarence's.

Tittering, Sarah came over and playfully ran a finger along Fargo's left ear. "You try to be nice to some people and look at how they act?" Like a child playing a game, she pranced completely around him, then wagged a finger in his face. "Naughty, naughty boy. I guess it's time to sever our relationship. You've outlived your usefulness." Pivoting to the southeast, she said over a shoulder, "Bring him."

Eight or nine pale specters seized Fargo and hauled him into the woods. He thrashed and bucked but there were too many of them. His arms and legs were firmly pinioned.

Sarah slowed so they could overtake her. "I'm sorry it came to this, handsome. To be honest, you were one of the best, ever. I had high hopes you would stick around for a spell."

"Glad to disappoint you," Fargo grated through clenched teeth.

"Don't be petty. It's unbecoming. Your last moments on this earth should be more dignified."

The trees thinned. The trail they had been following, a footpath no wider than a game trail, brought them to a short, pebble-strewn slope above a flat slab of rock.

He was carried out onto the slab, to the very brink. Below was a steep cliff, and at the base, jagged boulders.

"The fall is about two hundred feet, give or take a few," Sarah disclosed, leaning out. "Notice those white things at the bottom? They're bits and pieces of skeletons. This is how we've disposed of a few of the Air Breathers we caught."

Fargo regretted not shooting her when he had the chance. A drop from that height would break every bone in his body. Buzzards would pick them clean—unless coyotes got there first. No one would ever know what became of him. He would be just another frontiersman who had gone off into the wilds and never come back.

Sarah reveled in the moment. "No one bucks me, lover! Not ever! Not Charlie Vrittan, not my own husband, and certainly not you." She playfully rubbed his nose. "I'm accustomed to getting my own way."

Fargo had met women like her before. Beautiful but vain. Intelligent but self-centered. And above all, deadly. "Someone will stop you in time."

"Who? Vrittan? He's been trying for years. And the rest of the Air Breathers don't have the brains of a turnip among them." Sarah shook her head. "All the times they've tried to snare me, and couldn't! They don't even know about the secret tunnel in my root cellar."

"Moran and Boker should have shot you down that day they came to your place," Fargo said.

"You drove them off, remember?" Sarah rubbed it in. "Not that they would have, anyway. Charlie Vrittan frowns on harming women and children. He'd much rather take me alive."

Olivia Dixon had been right, Fargo reflected. Arvin had fed him a passel of lies. The real monster in those mountains wasn't Charlie Vrittan; it was the leering lovely in front of him.

"Enough idle chitchat," Sarah declared. "Before you leave this world, though, I think it only fair to inform you that I lied about the wagon train stock, too. The Utes didn't take our horses. I had them shot so no one could go for help until I was damn good and ready." She winked. "I haven't quite made up my mind about your pinto yet. Part of me wants him killed and butchered for the meat. But I might hold onto him for when the time comes to leave."

Fargo's blood boiled in simmering rage.

"Let's get this over with. I have things to do." Arvin stepped to one side. "Throw him off."

At that, the Dirt Breathers lifted Fargo and threw him over the cliff.

8

Desperate moments called for desperate deeds. .

As the pale-hued men and women lifted him to heave him over the precipice, Skye Fargo clutched the arm of a woman on his left and the faded brown belt of a man on his right. The next instant he was thrown over the edge. He held on as the woman screamed in terror and the man cursed lustily. Both started to slide toward the brink but were grabbed by their friends, arresting their plunge. And also arresting Fargo's. He dangled half over the cliff, but only for the few seconds it took for him to bunch his shoulder muscles, brace his legs, and hurl himself back up on top.

Confusion reigned among the Dirt Breathers. Many were holding onto the pair Fargo had grabbed. Before anyone could think to thwart him, Fargo had regained his footing and plowed into several Dirt Breathers on his left. Bowling them over, he took another long bound and was in the clear.

"Stop him, you idiots!" Sarah Arvin hollered.

It sent the whole menagerie howling after Fargo like so many rabid dogs. He reached the trees just a few steps ahead of them. Cloaked in ebony, he wove among the boles and brush with the skill of a black-tailed buck. A shot boomed, and a slug buzzed past. Fargo's own rifle was being used against him. So was the Colt. It cracked twice, but the shots went wide.

Hurdling a log, Fargo swerved to the right just as the Henry boomed again. He had gained about ten yards, but it wasn't enough. Barreling through a stand of saplings, he raced out the other side. Out of the night reared a thicket. Diving flat, he snaked into it and curled his legs to his chest.

Fargo had hardly frozen, when feet drummed in the darkness. Dirt Breathers raced past the thicket on either side. Some, though, slowed and probed the undergrowth. They communicated in grunts and other sounds more reminiscent of bears or buffalo than human beings.

A twig snapped within a few steps of where Fargo lay hidden. He glimpsed a pair of legs but dared not lift his head to see if the Dirt Breather was peering into the thicket. Any movement, however slight, might give him away.

There were more footsteps, and a dress swished loudly. "Spread out, damn you!" Sarah Arvin bawled. "He has to be around here somewhere!"

The Dirt Breathers began crisscrossing back and forth, covering every square foot of ground. Sooner or later it would dawn on one of them to check in the thicket. Fargo had hoped they would all keep on going, but it hadn't worked out that way. He placed his hands flat, about to slide out and make another bid to escape.

Suddenly huge, hide-covered feet came around the thicket from the other side. Clarence grunted excitedly, and for a moment Fargo thought he had been discovered.

"Air Breathers? Coming up the mountain?" Sarah translated the grunts aloud. "How many?"

Clarence grunted three times.

"Why would they risk being in the woods at night? They know the dark is our element." Sarah snapped her fingers. "I've got it! They must be hunting for Fargo." She uttered a short, sadistic laugh. "Since he's vanished into thin air, we'll make do and kill them instead."

A few more grunts and a gurgling whine imparted more information.

"You don't say?" Arvin said. "One of the townsfolk is a woman? That's mighty interesting. I wonder if it's her? Could I be so lucky? Let's go find out."

The blonde whistled shrilly. At her signal, the Dirt Breathers gathered from all points, and within moments she was leading them off down the mountain in the general direction of Vrittan.

Fargo waited until they were almost out of earshot then slid from the thicket and trailed them. He had a good idea who the woman Arvin mentioned must be, although he couldn't imagine why she had ventured so far from the safety of town.

The events of the previous few days were beginning to take a toll. Fargo's legs were stiff, his calf muscles prone to cramping. He had an ache in his gut and every so often his head would throb. He wasn't fully recovered yet from the desert. He had eaten his fill and caught up on his sleep, but it would be days yet before he was his old self.

The sounds ahead grew fainter. Not because Fargo was falling behind, but because Sarah and her band had slowed and were moving much more quietly. They must be getting close to the Air Breathers.

Circling to the left, Fargo went faster. He had to get around in front of the Dirt Breathers and warn Olivia Dixon and whoever was with her that they were climbing into an ambush. He had gone another twenty yards when he realized the Dirt Breathers weren't making any noise at all. They had gone to ground. As he drew abreast of where he believed they were concealed, he slowed in order not to give himself away.

Below, the trees gave way to a meadow. Tall grasses swayed in the breeze. And just stepping into the open were the three townspeople. Even at that distance Fargo recognized Dixon. Two men were with her, armed with rifles. They scoured the mountain above but paid no attention to the woods bordering the far side of the meadow. The very woods in which the Dirt Breathers were waiting.

Within seconds Dixon and the townsmen would be within range of Fargo's stolen Henry. He wasn't close enough to warn them without giving himself away. But he never hesitated. Cupping his hands to his mouth, he yelled, "Olivia! Go back! You're walking into an ambush!"

Fargo flung himself behind a tree as the Henry opened up. But whoever fired it didn't shoot at the Air Breathers. The shots were directed at him! With leaden hornets whining overhead, Fargo pivoted and dashed in among some pines. His Colt started cracking, a lesser echo of the Henry.

The two men from Vrittan responded in kind while retreating, Olivia shielded behind them.

Fargo smiled to himself. He had thwarted Sarah's plan. By now she must be mad enough to spit horseshoes. But his elation was premature. For suddenly a giant form reared up to the rear of Olivia and her friends. They didn't see it. They were too busy returning fire. Clarence tore into them like a grizzly into unsuspecting prairie dogs. One immense arm encircled Olivia's waist and lifted her bodily into the air while the other clubbed the two townsmen. Both folded like wet paper.

Into the meadow spilled the majority of the Dirt Breathers, Sarah bounding at their head and cackling in demented glee.

The rest of the pale killers swooped in Fargo's direction. Rising, he bolted due west. It would take him away from Dixon and her friends, but that couldn't be helped. Unarmed, he was no match for six or seven frenzied furies. He had to elude them. Afterward, he would circle back to help Olivia.

Or would he? The Dirt Breathers were ungodly fast. Sarah had sicced the fleetest of her followers on him, and soon two of them were so close, he could hear their heavy breathing. He was glad neither had a gun.

Fargo concentrated on outdistancing them. He stayed alert for obstacles: a boulder, a bush, a stunted tree were all avoided without mishap. But he was so intent on the ground that he failed to notice a low, thick tree limb until he was almost on top of it, and by then all he could do was throw an arm in front of his face and try to duck. It wasn't enough. The collision slammed him off his feet and flung him into the two Dirt Breathers nipping at his heels. Caught unaware, both were sent tumbling.

Fargo rolled as he hit, and pushed up into a crouch.

He was weaponless but far from defenseless. Out of the dark rushed a third Dirt Breather, and by shifting Fargo avoided the man's outstretched fingers and planted a solid blow to his pursuer's abdomen and another to his jaw.

Now was the time to get out of there. Fargo barreled toward the undergrowth, but a hand enfolded his ankle and brought him to a stop. He planted his other boot in the culprit's mouth, jerked his leg loose, and again attempted to reach cover. But another Dirt Breather latched onto his shoulders, seeking to hold him until the others could pile on.

Fargo had other ideas. He drove an elbow into the man's throat, and the Dirt Breather staggered but didn't go down. Tearing loose from the gold-crazed fanatic's grasp, he flicked a right cross that turned the man's leg to water. Then, spinning, he gained the brush a few steps ahead of onrushing Dirt Breathers.

Fargo exerted himself to his fullest but he was tiring. His body couldn't take much more. He had to give them the slip and he had to do it within the next minute or two or there was a very good chance he wouldn't live to see the dawn.

A tree trunk leaped out at him. Veering, Fargo avoided it and plunged into dense growth that tore at his buckskins and clung to his legs.

A hand fell on his left shoulder.

Fargo shrugged it off but the hand clamped down again. Reaching back, he grabbed the Dirt Breather's wrist, suddenly slowed, and threw all his strength and weight into an over-the shoulder toss.

The Dirt Breather managed a strangled screech of surprise that ended with the crunch of his head striking the wide bole of a pine.

Plunging ahead, Fargo ran until all sounds of pursuit dwindled and stopped. He was coated with sweat, and his legs were wobbly. Leaning against a fir, he breathed deep of the crisp night air and pondered his next move. He needed to recover the Ovaro, regain his weapons, and do what he could to save Olivia Dixon and the townsmen, but not necessarily in that order. Dixon and her friends were in immediate danger. They came first. But he needed a few minutes to catch his breath.

Fargo had to admit he sure did have a knack for getting into dangerous situations. It reminded him of the time a few years back when he had been seated around a saloon table in Denver with several old-timers, swapping tall tales about the old days. A reporter from a local newspaper had asked to sit in to take notes for an article. At one point the reporter had looked at them in wonder and asked how it was they had so many great adventures?

"Adventures" wasn't quite the word Fargo would use. Fighting hostiles, tangling with wild beasts, and being battered by the elements weren't his favorite pastimes. He never went out of his way to seek trouble; it always found him.

The problem was the frontier itself. West of the Mississippi River was no place for the timid. Violence was as much a part of daily life as breathing, and those who chose to live there had to accept that fact. Encountering Indian war parties, outlaws, and hungry grizzlies were normal occurrences. These things happened all the time.

Fargo increased his own odds by never staying in one place more than a few days. His wanderlust always drove him to see what lay over the next mountain range. And over the next range were always more cutthroats, more painted warriors, and more wild beasts. It was a never-ending cycle. Now here he was again, up to his neck in a predicament not of his own making.

Some frontiersmen might say to hell with it, go find the Ovaro and ride on out. He didn't owe Olivia Dixon anything. Nor the Air Breathers, for that matter. It wasn't his fight. But not Fargo. It wasn't that he saw himself as some sort of knight in shining armor. Quite the contrary. He avoided trouble whenever he could. But when it sought him out, when someone as vicious as Sarah Arvin tried to snuff out his life, it riled him. He didn't owe Dixon, but he sure as hell owed Arvin.

He would see it through to the end, come what may.

Fargo had never been a quitter. Never one to give up when things got rough. Nor was he the kind to turn the other cheek. When someone hit him, he hit them back. When someone tried to kill him, he planted them six feet under. And he didn't give a damn if it was a man—or a woman—on the other end of the barrel.

Fargo's legs had stopped shaking and he could breathe easily once again. Turning, he made for the meadow where he had last seen Dixon and the two townsmen. He couldn't predict what Sarah Arvin had in store for them, but he was sure she would want to gloat over Olivia a bit before killing her.

In all his travels Fargo had never met a female as outright brutal as Sarah Arvin. Few wives were so vicious as to have their own husbands slain. Few mothers could cut the tongues out of their own sons' mouths. Arvin had no conscience. No qualms about killing or using people to her own ends. Unless she was stopped, the toll of innocent lives lost and ruined would continue to climb. He wasn't going to let that happen.

It took longer than Fargo anticipated to reach the meadow. Dixon and her companions were gone, carted off by the Dirt Breathers to who-knew-where. Then the image of the white bones littering the base of the cliff seared him, and he knew, as surely as he was standing there, where the Air Breathers had been taken. Could he find it again in the dark? He remembered that the cliff was somewhere southeast of the mine entrance. But how far? He hadn't been paying a lot of attention.

Time crawled by as Fargo scaled slope after steep slope. His lungs were beginning to hurt and he was laboring for breath when voices filtered down through the trees. Slowing, he moved more cautiously. Soon he was rewarded with the sight of a score of Dirt Breathers ringing the cliff. At their center Sarah Arvin strutted back and forth in front of Olivia Dixon and Olivia's male companions. All three were on their knees.

Fargo crept closer. Sarah was raving about something or other and flapping her arms like an angry jay flapping its wings. A few more steps and he could hear her.

"—blame me for your brother's death! Johnny should have let well enough be! All these years you've held this grudge, and I'm sick of it!"

Olivia showed no fear. She held her head high, her chin tilted in defiance. "You always were good at making excuses for your atrocities," she calmly responded. "It's always someone else's fault. Never your own."

Sarah had a wild aspect about her. Wild, and undeniably savage. Here was no demure female, no pampered and tame product of civilization. She was as fierce as an Apache, as cold as a glacier. Snarling deep in her throat, she slapped Dixon across the face, rocking the smaller woman. "No one talks to me like that! But then, you never did know when to keep your silly mouth shut."

Olivia touched a finger to a corner of her bleeding mouth, and stared at the drops of blood. "Do what you will, Sarah. I won't keep quiet to appease you. There will come a time when you will be called to account for your crimes. My only regret is that I won't be around to see it."

Sarah suddenly bent and clasped the brunette's hand in earnest entreaty. "It's still not too late. Come over to our side, Olivia. Pledge yourself to our cause. Prove your loyalty by having your tongue cut out, and things between us will be like they were in the old days."

"You are out of your mind."

Again the lightning transformation took place. Rising up, Sarah growled like a she-cat and raked Olivia's cheek with her nails. "See? I tried! I offered you an olive branch and you threw it back at me."

Bloody furrows welled up on Olivia's flesh. She winced, then said softly, "Even if I agreed you were in the right, which you're not, and even if I could overlook all the horrible deeds you've done, which I can't, I would never, ever agree to having my tongue removed."

"It's not your whole tongue," Sarah declared. "We only cut off about half."

"As if that makes a difference," Olivia said sorrowfully, and gazed sadly at the Dirt Breathers. "To this day

I can't comprehend why they let you talk them into it. They must be as insane as you are."

"There you go again. Implying my sanity is the issue when the real issue has always been the gold, and how to divide it up. All I ever wanted was what was fairest for everyone. Charlie is the one who wouldn't listen to reason. Charlie is the one who insisted he deserved more than anyone else."

"Charlie is the one who found the mine."

"So? He couldn't dig out all the ore by himself. He couldn't transport it out of these mountains. Truth is, he needed us more than we needed him. His selfishness is to blame for the bloodshed. His pigheadedness was the real reason your brother, Johnny, died."

"There you go again," Olivia said.

Sarah swore and raised her hand to strike, but changed her mind and resumed pacing. "I can see there is no reasoning with you. I'm sorry, but what happens next is on your shoulders."

Out of the blue, Olivia inquired, "Is it true there are a lot of fumes down in the mine?"

"Eh?" Sarah's features scrunched in confusion. "Fumes? What the hell do they have to do with anything?"

"Charlie says there are a lot of fumes at the lower levels, where all the gold was found. Fumes that made him light-headed. Fumes that sometimes made him feel as if he were half-drunk."

Fargo recalled the faint odor of rotten fruit he had smelled in the tunnel leading to the pit.

"So?" Sarah snapped. "The lower levels stink to high heaven. What about it?"

"He believes the lower tunnels are filled with some kind of gas. A gas that can affect the mind." Olivia placed a hand on her former friend's knee. "Think about it. You and the rest of your people spent months down there digging out the bulk of the ore. Months cooped up in those narrow passages, breathing that foul smell. There's no telling what the gas did to you."

"Now who's insane?" Sarah asked, and chortled.

"Am I? That was about the time you decided your people should cut off their tongues, wasn't it? And also when you started killing women and children?"

"What's your point? That the gas changed us? That it warped us somehow?"

"Precisely," Olivia said, smiling as if she had made a breakthrough. "It turned the kindly Sarah Arvin I knew into the bloodthirsty killer you've become. You had your own husband murdered, for God's sake. The Sarah I once knew would never commit so foul an act."

Was it possible? Fargo asked himself. Could months spent in the bowels of the mine, breathing tainted air, have changed Arvin so drastically? Could it have driven her and the others to the edge of madness?

Sarah paced a few more times, then frostily stared down at her former friend. "Didn't it ever occur to you that maybe the woman you thought you knew wasn't the real me? Maybe my marriage wasn't as happy as you thought? Maybe the love had died a long time ago?" Her voice dropped until Fargo could barely hear her. "I never told you, did I, that Frank wanted to get rid of Clarence? He wanted to put our son in one of those homes for the mentally feeble."

"He never mentioned it to me," Olivia said, but Sarah appeared not to hear.

"Frank was sick and tired of always having to move. Of always having to put up with the stares and the fear. Everywhere we went it was the same. Children would take one look at Clarence and run off screaming. Grown women would look fit to faint. California was to be our last try at living a normal life. And if it didn't work out, I had a choice to make. Frank gave me an ultimatum. Either him or my son."

"No! Surely he wouldn't."

Sarah turned to Clarence and tenderly touched his chin. "I would die before I would let anyone take my boy from me. He can't help it if he's so hideous." Her face hardened and she poked a finger at Dixon. "You talk about blame. Who do I blame for my son's condition? Who do I hold to account for all his years of suffering? I'll tell you!" She poked the same finger at the stars. "I blame him. God Almighty! The cruelest of the cruel."

"You don't mean that."

Lunging, Sarah clutched Dixon by the throat. "Yes, I most certainly do! Bible-thumpers are forever telling us God is a god of love and mercy. Where was this vaunted love when my son was born? What did Clarence ever do to deserve coming into this world deformed?" She was shaking from the intensity of her emotions. "*He did nothing!* He was a baby. As innocent as innocent can be."

Olivia tried to reply but her breath was being choked off. She swatted at Arvin's forearm but Arvin apparently didn't feel the blows.

"That was the day I saw the light!" Sarah declared. "That was the day I realized the joke God has been playing on us since the dawn of time. He's not a god of love. He's a god of cruelty."

Fargo edged nearer. Something had to be done or Olivia would be strangled.

Suddenly Sarah stepped back and Dixon slumped over, wheezing and gasping and shaking her head. Her respite was short-lived. Arvin smacked the smaller woman across the top of the head and rasped, "So spare me your silly protests. This world is a living hell, and only those strong enough to fight it on its own terms make it through alive."

The older of the two townsmen finally had something to say. "With an outlook like that, no wonder you've shown us no mercy."

"Mercy is for weaklings, Higgins," Sarah said, and grunted at the Dirt Breathers. Five of them pounced on him. Higgins struggled, but he couldn't prevent the pale madmen from bearing him toward the cliff.

"Nooo!" Olivia Dixon sprang to her friend's assistance. She kicked one of the Dirt Breathers in the leg, kneed a second below the belt. Higgins pushed another off, and for a second it seemed he would break free. Then three more Dirt Breathers fell on him while three others restrained Dixon.

Fargo was in the open but as yet no one was aware of it. All eyes were fixed on the captives. He cast about for a weapon, for a fallen limb, a large rock, anything, and saw his Henry in the hands of a skinny Dirt Breather near the cliff. Another must have his Colt, and the toothpick, but he couldn't spot them. The Henry would do. Half-crouching to avoid being seen by Clarence, he circled to the left.

The Dirt Breathers were hauling Higgins toward the precipice.

Olivia Dixon was beside herself. "Please, Sarah, no! I beg you! He's never done you any harm! Don't do this!"

Sarah dismissed the appeal with a sneer.

"Please!" Olivia pleaded. "Kill me if you must, but let Higgins and Clark go. They only came along to protect me."

"Some protectors!" Sarah taunted, and gave a haughty toss of her golden hair. "Hasn't it sunk in yet I don't give a damn about them? Or about anyone else who sided with Charlie?"

"But this is wrong!"

"As if I care." Sarah laughed. "Weren't you the one who mentioned a short while ago that I had my own husband murdered? If I could kill Frank and not lose any sleep over it, do you honestly believe I would hesitate to kill these two slugs?"

Fargo was almost to the gap between the Dirt Breathers and the cliff edge. Another few seconds and he would be close enough to the man holding the Henry to spring.

"Dispose of them!" Sarah commanded

Bedlam erupted. The third Air Breather, Clark, had held back so far, but now he waded into the Dirt Breathers with his fists flying. He was a lot younger than Higgins, a brawny farmer who made up in raw strength what he lacked in skill. He scattered Dirt Breathers like straw in the wind. Dixon and Higgins were inspired to renew their own efforts, and fought using their hands, their feet, their teeth.

It was now or never. Fargo burst around the Dirt Breathers and over to the scarecrow holding the Henry.

The man was watching the uneven tussle. Grabbing the rifle, Fargo wrenched it loose, pivoted, and slammed the stock against the man's jaw. He only intended to knock the man down. Instead, the string bean tottered, his arms pinwheeling, and plummeted over the cliff. As he went over, he screamed.

All eyes now swung on Fargo. The pale apparitions surrounding him froze, including those battling Dixon and her friends.

Sarah Arvin smiled, a chilling blend of arrogance and triumph made all the more unnerving by her next comment. "Look who has saved us the trouble of hunting him down!"

Dirt Breathers started toward him and Fargo leveled the Henry. "Tell them to stay back or you'll lose a lot more of your followers." He didn't like how Sarah shook with silent mirth. "Don't you think I'm serious?"

"Quite the contrary," Sarah said. "But it's an empty threat." She laughed out loud. "You see, I know something you don't."

"What might that be?"

"Your rifle is empty."

9

Skye Fargo looked down at the Henry and worked the lever. A chill ran through him. The rifle was indeed empty. He still had a spare box of ammo in his pocket, but the moment he tried to reload, the Dirt Breathers would pounce.

Sarah Arvin laughed uproariously and was joined by some of the Dirt Breathers. "Not your lucky day, is it?" she baited him. "The gent you just sent to his Maker used up all the bullets earlier." Chuckling, she rubbed her hands together in wicked delight. "Here I was worried you might make it out of the mountains and alert the authorities, and you come waltzing right back into our clutches! You must feel mighty stupid right about now."

Fargo glanced at Olivia Dixon and gave a barely perceptible bob of his head. The empty rifle was a setback but it didn't change anything. They still had to fight their way out.

"Set down the rifle and we'll make this as painless as we can," Sarah offered. "One shove, and it will all be over before you know it."

"Then why don't you go first?" Fargo rejoined, and did the last thing any of them expected. Taking a quick step, he shoved Arvin toward the edge.

Sarah shrieked as she went over the lip. At the same instant, Clarence lunged and caught her around the wrist. He clung on as she frantically sought to acquire a handhold or a foothold to boost herself back up.

It distracted the Dirt Breathers. Several rushed to help the young giant, jostling one another in their anxiety. The men holding Olivia and Higgins hustled aside to get out of the way.

Fargo caught Clark's eye. The big farmer nodded, and side by side they lit into the Dirt Breathers, Fargo laying about him with the Henry's hardwood stock while Clark flicked his powerful fists. Momentary surprise worked in their favor. Like twin tornados sweeping aside chaff, they smashed the pair of pale devils holding Olivia to the ground, and then the three of them leaped to Higgins's defense.

The rest of the Dirt Breathers tore their gaze from Arvin and her giant son and rallied. Within heartbeats Fargo was hemmed in from three sides. Hands clutched at his arms, at his legs. Someone got an arm around his neck, and squeezed. He was on the verge of being pulled down.

Like a man gone berserk, Fargo reared up. Swinging the Henry right and left, he cracked it against a skull on one side, against a chalky face on the other. He never slowed, never relented. Spinning, twisting, dodging, swinging, he cleared a space in front of him and barreled toward the trees, shouting "Follow me!" to the Air Breathers.

Olivia, Clark, and Higgins were right behind him, raining fists and kicks on attacker after attacker.

Fargo had high hopes the four of them would make it. Then a pistol cracked. Whirling, Fargo saw Clark had gone down, a bullet hole in his forehead.

The Dirt Breather responsible was holding the Colt in a two-handed stance, and was now taking aim at Olivia.

Gripping the Henry by the barrel, Fargo whipped the rifle in a tight arc that shattered the man's teeth like so many brittle twigs. As the Dirt Breather fell, Fargo snatched the Colt from his limp fingers.

"Here!" Fargo tossed the rifle to Olivia, then fanned a shot that took a charging Dirt Breather low in the sternum and left him prone in the dirt. He shot another

Dirt Breather armed with a knife. The rest backpeddled. "Let's go!" he shouted, breaking for the vegetation, and glanced back to ensure the pair did likewise.

Olivia was using the Henry like a club. Higgins, doing his best to protect her, came last. When a burly character tried to get at Dixon from behind, Higgins drove the man off with a flurry of punches. But in the process he had to turn his back on several others.

Fargo saw steel glitter and opened his mouth to yell a warning, but the blade had slicked to the hilt. Higgins was dead before he crashed to earth, the knife jutting from between his shoulder blades. It was the toothpick. Triggering a round at the killer, Fargo took two swift steps and yanked it out.

Clarence had pulled Sarah up. She was screaming for her followers to stop them, but with eight or nine down, either dead or bleeding and bruised, the rest weren't too eager to close in.

Wielding the Arkansas toothpick as if it were a sword, Fargo cut a path through the remaining Dirt Breathers. The woods were so near, so inviting. Olivia at his elbow, he fled into the sheltering gloom, pausing at the tree line to fire a final shot to discourage the more persistent pursuers.

"Poor Higgins!" Olivia lamented as they scurried down the slope. "Poor Clark!"

"Now's not the time," Fargo advised. Any moment Sarah Arvin would rally the Dirt Breathers and the entire pack would streak after them. He listened for the crash and crackle of undergrowth, but half an hour went by without sign of them.

"Is it safe to stop yet?" Olivia puffed.

"I doubt it." Fargo guided her into the heaviest timber yet. Timber that soon ended at an erosion-worn gully. "Watch you don't fall," he cautioned, and half-leaped, half-slid to the bottom.

Dixon stumbled into him. To steady her, Fargo clasped her about the waist. The next thing he knew, her face was against his chest.

"It's all my fault," Olivia quietly sobbed. "They were

two of my best friends, and I got them killed. They wouldn't let me search for you alone."

"You can't blame yourself." Shoving the Colt into its holster, Fargo relieved her of the Henry. She gripped his shirt and cried without restraint in great, choking sobs. The heat her body gave off warmed him against the night's chill, and he could feel her firm breasts flush against his chest.

Not so much as a puff of wind disturbed the forest.

Fargo couldn't explain the Dirt Breathers' absence. There should have been some sign of them by now. He let Dixon weep herself dry. When she was done and stepped back, sniffling and wiping at her face with a sleeve, he ushered her to a flat spot and bid her sit. "We can rest a while longer yet."

Olivia draped her forearms over her knees and placed her forehead on them. "I'm sorry to break down like that. But Higgins was like a father to me. He was always willing to listen to my problems, always there when I needed him."

"Stop torturing yourself." To take her mind off it, Fargo knelt and asked, "Why did you come after me? Did Charlie Vrittan send you?"

Olivia dabbed at her eyes with her other sleeve. "It was my idea. I wanted to convince you to come back to town. To persuade you we never meant you any harm."

"Then why did those men threaten to break down your door to get at me?" Fargo responded. "Why did I have to fight my way out?"

"It was all a misunderstanding. You're the first outsider to make it here alive. They were excited. They wanted to talk to you, to get you to help us." Olivia paused. "And if you'll recollect, you were the one who resorted to violence first. Poor Sweeney will have a goose egg on his head for a month of Sundays."

"I'd like to believe you," Fargo said. Now that Sarah had revealed her true nature, it lent weight to Olivia's account.

"Come back with me, then. Talk to Charlie. Hear him out. That's all we ask."

"I don't know—" Fargo hedged. He still didn't trust them enough. The last time, he had barely made it out of town.

Olivia placed her small hands on his broad shoulders. "What can I do to convince you? What will it take?"

"There's nothing you can say or do," Fargo informed her. It was his decision, and his alone. And he would make it in his own good time.

"How about this?" Olivia said, and stretching up, kissed him full on the mouth.

It was so unexpected, Fargo didn't respond. Her lips were warm and soft and inviting, but the contact was all too brief. "What the hell was that for?"

"I will do whatever it takes to get you back down the mountain. I will even go so far as to offer my body to you in return for your promise to talk to Charlie." Olivia's cheeks darkened as she said it.

Fargo grinned at her embarrassment. "Do this kind of thing often, do you?"

"I've made love before, if that's what you mean," Olivia said defensively, and gripped his arm. "Don't take this so lightly. We're desperate. *I'm* desperate. I will do anything—and I do mean *anything*—to end this nightmare."

"It's sweet of you," Fargo said, patting her hand. "But what kind of *hombre* do you take me for?" He liked willing women as much as the next man, but he had never forced a woman into shedding her clothes and he wouldn't start now.

"I know absolutely nothing about you," Olivia conceded. "But if you're like most males I know, there is one thing you can never pass up." She kissed him again, harder than before. The tip of her tongue slid along his upper lip, a tempting taste of more to come.

This time it was Fargo who pulled back, and slowly shook his head. "This isn't necessary. Whether I go see Vrittan or not has nothing to do with you."

Olivia pressed against him, her strawberry lips parted invitingly. "What's wrong? Don't you like to make love?"

Fargo thought of the scores of women who could vouch for his never-ending hunger in that regard, and grinned.

"See? I knew you weren't taking me seriously." Olivia started to hitch at her shirt.

"Don't," Fargo said, grasping her wrist. Her desperation must be boundless. "This isn't the best time or place. We'll talk about it later. Right now I have a horse to find."

"A horse? I offer you my body and all you care about is your horse?" Olivia looked down at herself. "Do I need four legs and a tail?"

"You're as pretty as any woman I've ever met."

Olivia perked up considerably. "Really? Then I reckon I shouldn't be too upset." See coughed to clear her throat. "Is this the animal you were after in town?"

Fargo nodded. "My stallion. Sarah has him hidden somewhere, and I aim to find him." Standing, he helped her up, then moved off down the gully. The going was a lot easier than in the woods.

"After we find your horse, will you come with me to see Charlie Vrittan?"

"I'm still mulling it over. I'll let you know when I make up my mind."

In a few hundred yards the gully ended. From there they hiked northward at a steady pace, Fargo intent on reaching Arvin's cabin before sunrise. His legs were hurting again and he had a dozen new bruises from the battle with the Dirt Breathers, but he forged on, regardless.

"Tell me," Olivia broke her long silence. "What are women wearing nowadays?"

"Clothes," Fargo answered.

She laughed without restraint. "What *kind* of clothes? It might not be important to you, because you're a man, but women have more of an interest in that sort of thing. I can't tell you how many times I've daydreamed of buying new clothes. Or new shoes. I imagine the styles have changed quite a lot since '49."

Fargo could think of plenty of things more important to him than the latest fashions. But after years of being stranded, Olivia must be starved for the latest news. So he humored her. "Bonnets aren't as popular in cities and towns anymore. The ladies like to wear wide hats trimmed with lace and netting. Most dresses are made from silk, and the hems don't go clear down to the ground like they used to. Women are allowed to show their ankles now."

"In public?"

"In public. Women are also wearing fewer petticoats. About four or five years ago a new invention came out called the crinoline. It's made of flexible hoops and shaped like a bell, and women wear it around their hips in place of the petticoats. Some are so wide at the bottom, a man can't get anywhere near whoever wears them."

"My word. Flexible hoops, you say?" Olivia was quiet a minute. "How is it you know so much about female undergarments?"

"I've seen a few," Fargo said, and let it go at that.

"I haven't worn a dress in years," Olivia said longingly. "The last one I owned, I wore to a frazzle and ran out of thread to make repairs. I couldn't see imposing on any of the other women so I started wearing my brother's clothes."

"You look good in them."

"I do? No one has told me that in longer than I care to remember. Ever since the split there hasn't been much time for luxuries like romance. There was one fella from our wagon train, Sherman, his name was, who was sweet on me. But the Dirt Breathers got their hands on him and dragged him into the tunnels."

"It's high time to end the feud," Fargo observed.

"We never wanted it to start to begin with," Olivia said. "Charlie and I both begged Sarah to change her mind, but she refused to listen."

"She told me Vrittan refuses to have her killed?"

"That's Charlie for you. Too tenderhearted for his own damn good. We must have tried thirty or forty times to take her prisoner, but we were always foiled. I've been pushing Charlie to invade the tunnels to get this over with but he won't listen. He's afraid too many on our side will be killed. The last time we tried to reclaim the mine, we lost three good people. The mine entrances are all booby-trapped."

"I know about them," Fargo said, and thought of Sarah's root cellar. "What if I could show you an entrance that isn't booby-trapped?"

"It would be a godsend. We could penetrate deep into the Dirt Breathers' lair and wipe them out where they live." Olivia plucked at the back of his shirt. "Will you take me there?"

"After I find my horse."

Olivia muttered something, then declared, "What's so special about this darned critter? How can it be more important than the lives of dozens of men, women and children? The way you act, a body would think it was your best friend."

Fargo had never thought of the Ovaro quite like that but the comparison was appropriate. In a sense the stallion was his best friend. He could no more abandon it to Arvin's not-so-tender mercies than he could go on living without his internal organs. "If my horse dies, none of us may ever get out of here."

"Point taken," Olivia said testily. "I just pray it doesn't take long to find."

That made two of them.

Ahead rose the broken hills that flanked the cabin to the south. Fargo stuck to the open as much as possible so they could travel faster. By his reckoning they had less than an hour to go when Olivia posed another question.

"Do you honestly and truly think I look good in these clothes?"

"Any man with blood in his veins would think the same," Fargo assured her, glad his back was to her so she couldn't see his smirk. "You're a beautiful woman." He mentally counted to ten.

"I can't recall the last time a man said that to me. It does a girl's heart good to hear it more than once a blue moon."

"After you return to the States, men will fall all over

themselves to make your acquaintance," Fargo predicted. "You won't have any trouble making up for lost time."

Olivia giggled coyly. "Why, Mr. Fargo, you're such a flatterer. If I didn't know better, I'd swear you have something else on your mind besides finding your stallion."

"Let's just say that if you ever kiss me again like you did up the mountain, I won't be responsible for what I do," Fargo planted the seed he hoped would kindle her interest to new heights. "I held back out of respect for you before, but a man can only control himself so long around someone so lovely."

"Flatterer," Olivia repeated, sounding tremendously pleased.

Sometimes, Fargo mused, women made it much too easy.

Dawn was a couple of hours off when they gazed down on Arvin's homestead from the crown of the last hill. A question occurred to him that he should have asked sooner. "How long has Sarah been living there?"

"Going on seven or eight years now, I reckon."

"Why didn't your people burn her out and shoot her down. Without her, the Dirt Breathers might give up."

"You're forgetting Charlie. He refuses to 'stoop to her level,' as he puts it."

Fargo glanced at her. "After all Arvin has done? After all the deaths she's caused?"

"You've got to meet Charlie personally to understand. He's the kindest, sweetest man who ever lived. That's why so many of us objected, including Sarah's own husband, when she proposed stealing his gold out from under him. It just wasn't right."

"I look forward to meeting him." Fargo was sincere. Vrittan was the key to the whole affair, the one who had set it all in motion. If the man was all Dixon claimed, he deserved all the help he could get. At the moment, though, they had a more pressing concern. "I don't see my horse in the corral. And it won't be light enough to look for tracks for another hour or more. We should find some cover until then."

"Whatever you think is best."

Fargo entered a stand of pines. Toward the center was a small clearing buffered from the wind and carpeted with pines needles. "This will do. Get some rest if you want." Sinking onto his back, he placed his left forearm across his eyes and tried to relax. He heard a soft step and then the pressure of Olivia's shoulder against his. The clearing had to be ten feet in diameter yet she had lain right next to him. Shifting his arm, he peeked from under it.

Olivia was on her side, facing him. She had undone two more buttons on her shirt and was fussing with her hair. It wasn't her shoulder that was brushing against him. It was her bosom.

Fargo lowered his arm. "Something on your mind?"

Olivia stopped fussing and stammered, "No, no, whatever makes you say that?"

Fargo stared at the swell of her breasts, outlined against her shirt.

"It's a bit chilly," Olivia explained, "and you give off a lot of warmth." She paused. "Besides, you did say you found me attractive." She pouted as she said it, sounding as if her feelings were hurt.

"Very much so," Fargo admitted.

"Most men would be happy to have a woman lie so close to them," Olivia went on. "Why, practically every unmarried man in town, and even some of the married ones, have hinted they would love to be where you are right now. There's this one fella who won't stop pestering me no matter—"

"You talk too much," Fargo said, and reaching up, he pulled her face down to his. Her lips parted and he glided his tongue between them and swirled the tip around. When he broke the kiss, she was flushed and breathing heavily.

"Why did you do that?"

"You wanted me to." Fargo ran a hand through her silken hair and rimmed an ear with his fingertip.

"I did n—!" Olivia began, but caught herself. After a moment she grinned crookedly. "I would be a hypocrite if I pretended to be offended. Truth is, I haven't stopped thinking about you since we met."

"And I've been wondering how you would look shed of your clothes," Fargo mentioned, grasping a button.

"Wait." Olivia covered his hand with hers. "Let's make one thing clear. I'm not in love with you. Hell, I hardly know you. So don't get any harebrained notions about the two of us settling down somewhere and rearing a passel of sprouts."

"Damn," Fargo said, doing his best to appear disappointed. "And here I was fixing to propose."

Olivia jerked back, her lovely eyes widening, then realized he was joshing. Covering her mouth with a hand, she bowed her forehead to his chest and laughed a good three minutes.

Fargo's comment hadn't been *that* hilarious. He figured there had to be more to it, that maybe she was so used to men chasing her that for one to do the opposite had struck her funny bone. "I suppose if all you want to do is make love, my feelings won't be too hurt."

It triggered more laughter. Olivia's hair swished against his chin and her warm lips were inches from his neck. Below his belt a twitching began.

"I like you, Skye Fargo," Olivia said, straightening. "I like you a lot. You're handsome. You have a sense of humor. And you don't fiddle with a girl's feelings like most men do."

"That's me," Fargo said, taking her hand in his. "I'm all heart." With that, he boldly placed her palm on top of his hardening manhood.

"Oh!"

Fargo liked the hooded look of desire that came over her. He liked how her mouth puckered hungrily and she ran her pink tongue along her full lips. She leaned against him and slid her leg across his.

"I should warn you, mister," Olivia said huskily. "It's been a while since I was with a man. I might break you in half."

"Promises, promises," Fargo said, and without further

small talk, covered her breasts with his hands. She shuddered as he squeezed them—hard—and pinched her nipples through her shirt and undergarment.

"Yessss," Olivia panted. She turned her head from side to side, her hair spilling over her shoulders. "It's been too long. I'd almost forgotten how good it feels."

Suddenly sounds intruded, faint sounds from the direction of Arvin's cabin. Putting a finger to her mouth to shush her, Fargo slowly rose. He motioned for her to stay there and stalked off through the pines to where he had an unobstructed view of the homestead. Light blazed in the windows, and there was a commotion inside. Someone was talking in a loud voice amid a lot of thumping and pounding. He was much too far off to hear what was being said but he was sure the speaker was a woman. It had to be Sarah Arvin. Evidently she had returned through the tunnels, bringing Dirt Breathers with her. Whatever they were up to would keep them occupied a while, from the sounds of things.

That suited Fargo just fine. He still had time to kill until daylight. He turned to go back and nearly collided with Olivia, who had come up behind him. "I wanted you to stay at the clearing."

"Have you ever met a woman yet who listens when a man tells her to do something?" was the brunette's response. She took a step past him and rose onto the tips of her toes. "What on Earth are they up to down there?"

"Your guess is as good as mine."

"Should we sneak on down for a look-see?" Olivia proposed.

Fargo shook his head. He couldn't risk being spotted, not until after he recovered the Ovaro. The stallion came before all else.

"I guess you're right. We wouldn't be able to see much, anyway, with the windows covered like they are. We'll have to wait until dawn." Olivia's shirt was still partly unbuttoned, revealing the delightful contours of her twin mounds.

The cabin door opened and for a moment someone—

possibly Sarah Arvin—was silhouetted against the lamp light. She stood there for half a minute or so, then moved back inside and closed the door.

"What was that all about?" Olivia wondered.

"Who cares?" Fargo looped an arm around her slim waist and pulled her close. His other hand on her pert bottom, he guided her over against a tree and pressed hard against her. "Now where were we?"

"You were telling me how much more fond of horses you are than women."

"I never said any such thing and you know it," Fargo said.

"My grandma used to say the proof is in the pudding." Olivia undid another of her buttons. "So prove it, big man."

10

Skye Fargo had learned never to prejudge a woman's passion by her size. Sometimes the smallest bundles were firebrands of lust and desire. Olivia Dixon was such a bundle. The instant his mouth glued to hers and his left hand covered a ripe breast, she surged against him like a wave breaking on a rocky shore. Her right leg wrapped around his. Her hands were everywhere at once, exploring, caressing. Her mouth was a bonfire, and her fiery kisses about took his breath away.

"So long," Olivia breathed when they parted for air. "So very, very long."

Fargo finished undoing the buttons and slid her shirt off. Her chemise was loose enough for him to expose her exquisite breasts in all their sensual glory. Bending, he latched his lips onto a nipple and swirled it with his tongue. It caused her to press her hands against the tree and arch outward. With his other hand he cupped her bottom and slid a finger between her legs.

Olivia whimpered. "Wet! Getting so wet!"

Fargo couldn't wait to see for himself. But he dallied at her breasts a while, lathering each in turn and sculpting them as if they were clay. For her part, Olivia hitched and tugged at his buckskin shirt until he took the hint and slid it off. Her eyes narrowing lustfully, she ran her hands over his corded chest and abdomen.

"Look at all these muscles! It's like rubbing a washboard!"

Tucking at the knees, Olivia lowered her mouth to his stomach and lavished wet kisses on it. Her tongue moistened his navel. Continuing to slide downward, she unbuckled his belt and pried at his pants. Fargo went to help her, but she swatted his hand aside and in no time had them down around his knees.

A lump formed in Fargo's throat. It was he who gasped at the moist contact, and who groaned when she licked him from stem to top and back again. Her warm fingers cupped him, low down, and the world around them danced and spun.

Some women, Fargo had learned, wouldn't touch a man there if their life depended on it. They were usually the ones who lay like bumps on a log and let the man do all the work. Other women, like Olivia, had no such inhibitions. They enjoyed lovemaking to the fullest and worked as hard at exciting the man as the man did at exciting them.

Olivia's long fingernails delicately scraped Fargo's sensitive inner thighs, and it was all he could do to keep from exploding. Gripping her hair, he pulled her up across his stomach until their mouths met. She was liquid honey. He stroked her neither region and could feel the dampness through her pants.

"I want you so much!"

The need was mutual. Swiftly, Fargo stripped off her jeans and underthings, and stood back to admire her. Awash in starlight, she was perfection itself. Her breasts were curved like sabers, her belly wonderfully flat, her thighs superb. His mouth watered at the sight of the thatch at their junction, and he quickly removed his boots and kicked out of his pants.

Olivia was fascinated by his jutting pole. "There's a lot more to you than I ever imagined. I thought you said your horse was the stallion!"

Grinning, Fargo pulled her close and kissed her hard. Her nails found his shoulders and scraped down over his back to his buttocks. Internal sparks shot through him, sparks that flared into blazing desire when she cupped her breasts and said in a sultry purr, "Like what you see?"

Squeezing her right breast, Fargo backed her against the tree and inhaled her tongue. Simultaneously, he thrust a hand between her velvet thighs and rubbed his forefinger across her wet valley. She quivered deliciously. When his finger rubbed her swollen knob, a low moan bubbled from her throat.

"I want you so much!"

"So you keep saying," Fargo responded. Sliding his calloused hands under her arms, he began to lift her off the ground. "Let's find out exactly how much."

"What are you doing?" Olivia asked, bewildered. She glanced down at her feet, suspended inches in the air, and rising higher inch by gradual inch, and comprehension dawned. "Oh my! Are you sure you're up to this?"

Her breasts were now as high as Fargo's mouth. Sucking on her left nipple, he slowly shifted so she was aligned directly above his pulsing member. He drew back to whisper in her ear, "You might want to bite your lip to keep from crying out."

"Oh, please. I'm a grown woman. It's not as if I haven't made love before."

"Ever done it like this?" Fargo retorted. And with a downward thrust of his arms coordinated with a smooth upward thrust of his hips, he rammed up into her, clear to the base of his member.

Olivia flung back her head. Her mouth gaped to scream but no scream came out. Instead, she clenched her teeth and trembled from head to toe like an aspen leaf in a summer storm. Her nails sank deep into his back.

Wrapping her smooth legs around his waist, Fargo held onto them and commenced a rocking motion. Up onto his toes he would go, then slowly sink back down. He buried his face between her breasts and kneaded her squirming bottom.

Olivia's inner walls clung to him, wreathing his manhood in pleasure without peer. "I can't hold off much longer, lover," she told him, her eyes smoldering. "I just can't. I'm sorry."

Fargo wondered why on earth she was apologizing. Firming his hold on her legs, he drew himself almost out, then slammed up and in. It had the desired effect.

In a frenzy of wanton abandon, Olivia Dixon ground herself against him, her hands on his shoulders for leverage. Her eyes and mouth were shut. With each stroke her nostrils flared and she would whimper or sigh or dig her nails a little deeper.

The shimmering stars overhead, the brisk wind on his bare skin, a willing woman sharing his climb to the heights of release. Life never got any better, Fargo mused. All he needed to make it complete was a full bottle of whiskey and a soft bed to collapse on afterward.

"Oh! Oh!" Olivia suddenly exclaimed, and bit his shoulder.

Her explosion was everything Fargo hoped it would be. She bucked and heaved, clawed and scratched, quaked and gushed. And when she was done, when she sagged limp and spent, thinking it was over, Fargo held her shoulders and looked deep into her opening eyes.

"Dear God! You didn't—?"

Fargo let his actions speak for him. He thrust up into her again and again, not too fast and not too slow, pacing himself so when his explosion finally came, he would enjoy it that much more.

Olivia's features betrayed bewilderment but only briefly. Smiling in anticipation, she matched his upward thrusts with downward thrusts of her own.

The urgent craving for release grew and grew. Through sheer force of will Fargo delayed it as long as he could. Then came the crucial moment. Olivia shuddered and cried, *"Ahhhhhhhh!"* He felt her spurt, felt her womanhood contract around his manhood, and his willpower was no longer enough.

The night dissolved in a showery haze of cascading colors. Fargo's body kept mechanically pumping while he soared on currents of pure pleasure. His groans mingled with hers. Their mouths joined one final time as they eased to the ground and slumped against each other, both totally spent.

Fargo closed his eyes but refused to fall asleep. He still had a horse to find. Too drowsy to budge, he didn't move until the warble of a songbird heralded the onset of a new day. He noticed a slight brightening of the eastern sky. There wasn't much light yet, but more than enough for him to locate his clothes and boots and gunbelt and sluggishly don them.

Olivia had drooped onto one side, her hands sufficing for a pillow. Fargo had half a mind to let her sleep. But given their proximity to the cabin, he knelt and gently shook her until she stirred.

"Sorry to wake you. It's almost time to head out."

Olivia mumbled and smacked her lips but didn't open her eyes. He shook her again and she rolled over so her back was to him and curled into a ball.

Fargo was on the verge of hauling her to her feet when a noise from the cabin brought him to his own. The door was open and half a dozen Dirt Breathers had emerged, Clarence foremost among them. Sarah Arvin had stepped outside as well. She was issuing instructions, but what they were, Fargo couldn't guess. He saw Arvin point to the northwest a few times. Then Clarence and the others filed off, moving rapidly, perhaps so they could reach their destination before the sun rose. Arvin went back inside and slammed the door behind her.

Turning to Dixon, Fargo slipped his hands under her arms and sat her up. "Rise and shine, beautiful. It's almost sunrise and we have a lot to do."

Olivia's eyes cracked open and focused on him in mild resentment. "Let me be, damn it. I need another eight to ten hours sleep."

"I can't leave you here alone," Fargo said. "There's no telling who might come by."

"Don't you fret none," Olivia persisted. "The Dirt Breathers rarely stray abroad during the day. They can't stand the sun. It hurts their eyes too much."

"You're safer with me." Fargo had her erect, but her legs were so much mush and she made no effort to straighten on her own.

"Please, good looking. We were up almost all night

and I'm plumb tuckered out. I need more rest or I'll be no use to you whatsoever."

She had a point, there. "All right," Fargo reluctantly conceded. "You can sleep until I get back. But you have to put your clothes on first and hide back in the bushes where no one can see you."

"You want me to get dressed? I barely have the energy to lift my little finger." Olivia batted her long eyelashes at him. "Would you be a dear and help me?"

"Women," Fargo said under his breath, and gathered up her clothes. She had him shake each garment before she would consent to put it on. When it came time for her shirt, she yawned and drooped and only raised her arms a few inches.

"I'm sorry. I'm so tired I can't stay awake."

Fargo raised her arms the rest of the way. When he was done, he gently lowered her onto her back and tugged her pants on. It took some doing since she had fallen asleep and he had to keep lifting her legs to inch the pants higher until they were at her waist. Lastly, he slipped on her worn shoes, and sat back. "It's a good thing you weren't wearing a corset and petticoats," he grumbled aloud. "This would have taken forever."

Fargo had to search a few minutes to find a suitable spot in the underbrush. He trampled some weeds, then deposited Olivia and folded her arms in front of her. She dozed blissfully on; an angel in repose.

Dawn was looming as Fargo finally made his way toward the corral. Circling to come up on it from the rear, he moved from tree to tree and bush to bush. The lamps in the cabin had been extinguished and no sounds came from inside. He construed that as a possible sign the Dirt Breathers had gone back underground.

Even so, Fargo didn't show himself until he had no other recourse. The Henry tucked to his shoulder, he dashed to the rails, and squatted. Sidling along them to the gate, which was open, he scoured the area for tracks. The ground was hard, compacted dirt, but it still bore prints. Someone wearing narrow, square-heeled shoes had led the stallion off into the mountains. The size and shape were typical of a woman. So were other tracks, inside the corral. All made by the one person who spent more time there than anyone else; Sarah Arvin.

The hoofprints, Fargo saw, went off in the same direction Clarence had gone not all that long ago. He started to follow, then, on an impulse, crept to the side of the cabin and over under the window. The burlap curtains were drawn. He couldn't see inside, but he did hear the rumbling sound of someone snoring. Placing his ear to the burlap, he established it wasn't just one person. Several people were snoring all at once. Dirt Breathers, he reckoned. The cabin was packed with them. But why were they holing up there instead of down in the mine? The answer could wait.

Quietly backing away, Fargo jogged to the northwest. The sun's radiant crown was bringing light and warmth to the world. Soon it would be full daylight. He paralleled the hoofprints, and Clarence's more recent monstrous tracks, for three-quarters of a mile. At that point the giant and the other Dirt Breathers had wound between a pair of low hills and entered a boulder-strewn gorge. Long shadows cast by towering stone cliffs hundreds of feet high shrouded it in perpetual gloom.

Fargo could have heard a pebble drop, the air was so still. Clarence had gone straight on up the middle of the gorge but Fargo chose to hug the base of the cliffs on the right where the shadows were deepest. He had seldom been so happy in his life as he was when, five minutes later he spotted a spring-fed grotto at the far end, and tethered near the spring, the Ovaro.

Also nearby were Clarence and seven Dirt Breathers. The latter were huddled near the back wall, grunting and gesturing, while Clarence was occupied with patting the stallion and feeding it clumps of grass. Since only five Dirt Breathers had been with Clarence when he left the cabin, Fargo figured the other two had been there all along, watching over the stallion.

Hunkering, Fargo waited. One by one the Dirt Breathers moved to the back wall and turned in. Presently only Clarence was left, but he showed no inclination to bed down. Quite the contrary. After petting the pinto, he prowled the grotto like a great bear and repeatedly gazed off down the gorge. Maybe he was expecting his mother to show up. Or maybe he was worried about her welfare.

Lying on his stomach, Fargo resigned himself to a long wait. The sun appeared above the high cliffs, filling the gorge with sunshine. Clarence continued to pace. Just when Fargo was beginning to think the giant would stay awake all day, Clarence grunted, shuffled to the rear, and laid down.

Fargo stayed where he was for another quarter of an hour to ensure the giant was asleep. Then, on cat's feet, he slunk toward the spring. He was twenty feet out, pressed low against a boulder, before he noticed the Ovaro's eyes were no longer bandaged. They were wide open, and much of the swelling had gone down. Whatever Sarah had used had worked wonders.

Suddenly the stallion's head rose, its nostrils flaring. Fargo knew it had caught his scent and he hoped it wouldn't whinny and wake up the Dirt Breathers. He preferred to avoid a clash if he could. He only wanted to get the pinto and get the hell out of there. By day's end he would be well on his way out of these godforsaken mountains, and by the end of the week he should reach the nearest army post.

Fargo would personally lead the army troops back. He was anxious to see the look on Sarah Arvin's face as she was taken into custody. Hell, he might even attend her trial to hear the judge sentence her to life in prison. She deserved to hang but women were rarely sent to the gallows. It wasn't considered proper.

Fargo eased around the boulder, took a step, and froze. One of the Dirt Breathers had abruptly sat up. Fixing the Henry's front sight on the man's torso, he braced for an outcry. But the man merely scratched under the deer hide he wore, rubbed his grizzled chin, and plopped back down.

The Ovaro was watching Fargo intently. It started to lift a leg to stomp a hoof, but lowered it without making any noise.

Fargo quickly crossed the open space and covered the

stallion's muzzle with his left hand. Impulsively, he threw an arm around its neck, then stooped and yanked at the crude stake to which the reins were tied. Someone had pounded the thing in deep. Setting down the Henry, he seized hold with both hands, planted his boots, and pulled. The stake wouldn't budge. Exerting every sinew, his lips compressed, he tried again, without success.

Unfurling, Fargo debated his next move. To loosen the stake required hitting it with a rock. But doing that would wake up the Dirt Breathers. Sinking onto his left knee, he drew the Arkansas toothpick. He could cut the reins and still have enough left to ride. Later on he would replace them.

Two slices and the task was done. Replacing the knife, Fargo reached for the Henry. Suddenly a suggestion of movement behind him made him glance over his shoulder.

Creeping toward him, a club elevated to strike, was a stocky Dirt Breather. The man was streaked with dirt and wore clothes with more holes and rips than any amount of sewing could ever stitch up. His beady, glittering eyes were lit with bloodlust, and his thick lips drawn back over yellowed teeth.

The instant Fargo glanced back, the man snarled and sprang. Pivoting, Fargo fired from the hip. The blast pealed like thunder in the grotto's confines, and the would-be killer was catapulted backward as if kicked by a Missouri mule.

At the shot, the rest of the Dirt Breathers scrambled up. Including Clarence, who took in the situation at a glance, and rushed to thwart the rescue.

A single step brought Fargo alongside the Ovaro. Clutching the stallion's mane, he swung astride its bare back, reined around, and lit out of there as if all the demons of the pit were after him. Which wasn't far from the truth. Braying and growling like a pack of feral dogs, the Dirt Breathers gave chase. Two were remarkably fast, and before Fargo could bring the Ovaro to a trot, they overtook him, one on either side, and grabbed at his legs.

Fargo smashed the Henry's stock into the snarling visage of the first and twisted to take care of the other. But the man jerked his head back, evading the blow, and lunged higher to clamp his arms around Fargo's waist. His intent was clear; to tear Fargo from the stallion and hold him until the rest caught up.

The Ovaro rapidly gained speed. Again Fargo swung the stock and clipped the Dirt Breather's shoulder. A loud grunt warned him another one was almost on top of them, and a hasty look confirmed it was Clarence.

"Get off me, damn you!" Fargo growled, and smashed the rifle into the Dirt Breather's mouth. The man sagged and fell just as Clarence leaped and a jab of Fargo's heels sent the Ovaro out of reach.

Both Dirt Breathers tumbled to the dirt and howls of frustration rose from the rest of the madmen.

Fargo held to a gallop until the gorge was well behind him. He still had to reclaim his saddle, bedroll, and saddlebags. The last two were in Arvin's cabin, last he knew, while his saddle was still draped over the top rail of her corral.

The Ovaro was eager to stretch muscles too long unused. Fargo gave the stallion its head and in what seemed like no time at all the cabin came into view. Reining into the trees, he gave it a wide berth to check on Olivia Dixon. He took it for granted she was still asleep. The sun was only an hour and a half high and she had been exhausted. But when he approached the spot where he left her and softly called her name, there was no reply.

"Olivia?" Fargo repeated, sliding down. Considering how hard it had been to wake her up earlier, he wasn't concerned until he reached the weeds he had trampled for her to lie on—and found her gone.

"Olivia?" Roving to either side, Fargo came on more trampled undergrowth. Not much further on were tracks. Enough to enable him to reconstruct the series of events, and to provoke him into cursing a blue streak.

Four Dirt Breathers had come on Olivia while she slept. It must have happened shortly after he left, and right before the sun rose. They had converged from all sides so she had no chance to get away, then dragged her, kicking and fighting, toward the cabin. Scrape marks testified to how fiercely she had resisted.

Since Fargo had no intention of letting the stallion out of his sight, he turned to climb back on.

"Don't move, mister!"

Several guns hammers clicked, convincing Fargo to do as he had been instructed, as out of the vegetation strode seven men and a pair of women. Two of the former he recognized. Moran and Bokor. The whole party had been in hiding the entire time, watching him.

"Drop your guns," commanded their leader, someone who had come up behind him.

"Like hell," Fargo said.

"Be reasonable. Or would you rather have gunplay?"

"You won't risk hitting my horse." At Fargo's mention of the Ovaro, Moran and Bokor and the rest of those covering him glanced anxiously at one another. "You don't dare kill your only hope of reaching the outside world." Confident they wouldn't shoot, Fargo rotated, seeking the person who had addressed him. But no one was there.

"A little lower, mister."

Glancing down, Fargo was unable to conceal his surprise. Before him stood a grey-beard who couldn't be more than three feet tall. The man's attire consisted of altered homespun clothes and a floppy hat. From under the brim peered frank blue eyes in which there wasn't a trace of ill will.

"Don't tell me," Fargo said. "I finally have the honor of meeting Charlie Vrittan."

"Flattery will get you everywhere, sir," the old prospector rejoined with a broad grin. He had a sincere, friendly air about him that lent the impression he didn't have an unkind bone in his body. "I am indeed the fool in question, much to my eternal regret." Vrittan offered a knobby hand.

Fargo shook it and was impressed by the small man's strength. "Olivia told me everything. I know you're not to blame for what happened."

"On the contrary," Charlie said, "I was the one who brought these good people here. Were it not for me, they would all be in California, fulfilling their dreams." Pushing his floppy hat back, he contemplated the group who had accompanied him. "Each and every one of these fine people has lost someone they loved. A friend, a wife, a husband, a child. And I'm the idiot who brought it about. Me, and all that damnable gold. It's unfortunate the mine didn't cave in on me before I ever set eyes on them."

The prospector's honesty was refreshing. "You're here after Olivia Dixon, I reckon," Fargo deduced.

"I tried to stop her from going after you until morning, but she wouldn't listen," Charlie said. "She insisted you were the answer to our prayers and wanted to set things straight so you wouldn't think ill of us. Two fellas went with her. Higgins and Clark. You haven't seen them, by any chance?"

Fargo related the fate of the two men.

"Two more souls I must account for," Charlie said, and wearily rubbed his chin. "Will there never be an end?"

Fargo imparted the rest of the bad news. "Olivia has been taken by the Dirt Breathers. I was about to go after her when you showed up."

Charlie gazed toward the cabin. "I should have listened to the others and made maggot bait of Sarah Arvin years ago. But I never gave up hope of finding a peaceable solution. All I ever wanted was to help these people, not turn them against one another."

"Why *did* you offer those emigrants a stake in your gold?" Fargo asked the question that had been nagging at him since the very beginning. "To help you mine it, like Arvin claimed?"

"Is that what she told you?" Charlie sadly sighed. "I'm an old man, hoss. I could never spend all the gold I found if I lived to be a hundred. So I figured I'd invite some other folks to share in my good fortune. When the right wagon train came along, one with a lot of families, good people, I thought, who could use the gold a lot more than I ever could, well—" He shrugged, then looked up. "It's hard to believe so much suffering and bloodshed stemmed from the best of intentions."

"It's time to end it," Fargo said.

"I know. I know. I've been too considerate, too merciful, for far too long." Charlie pulled his hat back down. "But I'm not like Sarah. I don't like to kill. I've avoided it at all costs where possible and asked those with me to follow my example. To their credit, and their misery, they have."

"There comes a time when a man has to make a stand," Fargo declared. Swinging onto the stallion, he cradled the Henry. "Like it or not, killing time is here."

11

From behind a tree twenty-five yards from the cabin, Skye Fargo studied the dwelling for signs of life. The door was closed, the curtains were drawn. He heard nothing to indicate anyone was inside. It appeared to be empty, deserted. But he couldn't shake a vague premonition it wasn't.

"What are we waiting for?" Charlie Vrittan asked. "It's broad daylight. Even if some of the Dirt Breathers are in there, the sunlight will blind them when we kick in the door."

Some of the others nodded. They were impatient to do something.

"That's right," Moran chimed in. "Bokor and me can go bustin' on in there before those devils know what hit 'em." He glanced at Bokor, who grinned and hefted a Sharps. "Just say the word, Charlie. The longer we wait, the worst it's bound to be for Olivia."

"There's no telling what those monsters are doing to her," mentioned a woman old enough to be Dixon's mother.

Fargo would rather they take it nice and careful, but he didn't object when Charlie Vrittan nodded and gestured.

"Go ahead, Moran. But Bokor and you be careful, hear? We've already lost Higgins and Clark. We can't afford to lose one of you, too. Remember how devious and deadly Sarah's bunch can be. If it's an ambush, get right back out again. We'll cover you."

The pair crouched, glanced at each other, then raced

toward the cabin in a zigzag pattern to make themselves harder to hit.

"I only pray the Dirt Breathers haven't taken Olivia underground," Charlie somberly commented. "Down there, they are in their element. They know those tunnels even better than I do."

Moran and Bokor reached the cabin. Moran had said something to Bokor as they covered the final ten yards, and now they lowered their shoulders and slammed into the plank door side by side. It buckled under their combined impact. The next moment they were inside, swallowed by darkness. Several seconds of silence ensured.

"I reckon no one was in there," one of the other Air Breather's commented.

Just then a hellacious racket raised the rafters. Shouts and curses mixed with bloodcurdling screams and fierce shrieks. The Sharps thundered. So did Moran's revolver.

"They're in trouble!" Charlie cried, and leaped from concealment. "Come on! We've got to help them!"

In Fargo's opinion Vrittan was compounding one mistake by making another, but he charged toward the cabin with the rest. They hadn't covered a third of the distance when the uproar abruptly ceased. He took several more loping strides when suddenly the burlap curtains parted and a rifle muzzle was shoved out. Instantly, it spat smoke and lead.

An Air Breather close to Charlie clutched at a shoulder and spun halfway around.

"Take cover! Take cover!" Vrittan hollered, springing to help the wounded man. "They were waiting for us! It was a trap!"

The snout of another gun protruded from the shadowy doorway, and whoever held it blasted away.

Fargo backpedaled, returning fire as he retreated. He put two slugs into the center of the curtains and sent two more into the door jamb within inches of the second gun. Both weapons were jerked back. The Air Breathers regained cover without anyone else being wounded or slain.

The man who had taken a slug in the shoulder was

bleeding but not severely hurt. The bullet had penetrated just below his collar bone, and exited out his upper back without severing a major artery or breaking bone.

"You were lucky, Fred," Charlie told him while one of the women tore a makeshift bandage from her own shirt. "You lie here and rest while we take care of things."

"Like hell," Fred responded. He wasn't much over twenty and had a lantern jaw and big, bony hands. "Moran and Boker are my friends, and Olivia is like a sister to me. I'm not sitting the rest of this out."

The old man smiled and affectionately patted Fred's arm. "Your father would be so proud of you if he were still alive. You can help, but I don't want you taking any reckless chances. I refuse to lose anyone else. Preserving your lives is more important than getting revenge."

Fargo realized more than ever why Charlie Vrittan was held in such high esteem by those who had taken his side in the dispute. The old-timer was as decent a human being as could be. As decent, in fact, as he originally thought Sarah Arvin was. Yet they couldn't be more different if they tried. One was the epitome of goodness, the other harbored every wickedness known to man in her heart.

"Look!" one of the women cried, pointing at the cabin.

A white pillow case was flapping in the doorway.

"They want to parley," Charlie said, and rose to go. "Cover me in case it's another of their damnable tricks."

Fargo fell into step beside him. "You're not going alone."

The person waving the pillow case stepped outside. It was Sarah Arvin. As arrogant as ever, she bestowed a look of smug contempt on Vrittan. "When will you learn, you miserable dwarf, that I can outthink you any day of the week? I knew you'd try to rescue sweet Olivia and had a reception waiting."

"Is she still alive?" Charlie asked.

"I've slapped her around some to put her in her place, but that's all," Sarah disclosed, and shifted her attention to Fargo. "You're even more like that stallion of yours than I thought. Some of my boys saw you and her lying together, buck naked." Sarah laughed bitterly. "So tell me, lover. Now that you've had both of us, which of us was better?"

Fargo refused to answer.

"Cat got your tongue?" Sarah teased. "Very well. Play the gentleman. It won't change anything. In the end the little bitch will get hers. So I hope she enjoyed herself with you as much as I did. It's the last lovemaking she'll ever experience."

Charlie Vrittan was stupefied by the revelation. "You bedded bo—" he gaped at Fargo, then checked himself and shook his head. "Forget all that for the moment. Where are Moran and Bokor, Sarah? Are they alive?"

"Moran is," Arvin replied. "He's lost a few teeth and his nose is broken, but he's a lot better off than Bokor, who is on the floor next to my table with an axe sticking out of his head."

"Damn you," Charlie said. "Is there no quenching your infernal bloodlust?"

"He got what was coming to him, you pompous old goat. Either would have killed me given half the chance." Sarah crumpled the pillow case and angrily flung it into Vrittan's face. He made no attempt to catch it and it fell at his feet. "But then you've always been a hypocrite, haven't you, Charlie? Always pretending to have our best interests at heart when you were only concerned with your own."

"My offer to share the gold was genuine."

"You offered us a pittance, you old bastard," Sarah spat. "Too bad for you that I had more gumption than the rest. I was willing to fight for more. And now I have complete control of the mine, the gold, everything." She quirked her lips at Fargo. "That includes your horse, handsome. Which I've decided to hold onto until it's time for me to bid these mountains so long."

"Then you won't be going anywhere," Fargo responded, and pointed off through the trees to where the Ovaro was tethered by the creek.

Sarah gave a start and took half a step. "You got him

back? How? What about Clarence and the men I sent to keep watch?"

"I took the pinto right out from under their noses," Fargo rubbed it in. "And your son is still alive, last I saw." He had to keep in mind the youth might show up at any minute, and stay on the lookout.

Once again the terrible transformation occurred. Sarah's features contorted into a flinty mask of unleashed hatred. "So you think you've gotten the better of me, do you? You think you've spoiled my plans? But I'm nothing if not adaptable. Just ask the dwarf, here." Suddenly scurrying indoors, she said over a shoulder, "Don't go anywhere. I'll be right back."

"I don't like the sound of that," Charlie said quietly.

Fargo didn't like the rifle muzzle trained on them from the window, or the revolver visible from a few feet inside pointed squarely at his chest. He heard a voice raised in protest, then the sound of a slap. Out of the murky interior stalked Arvin. This time she had Moran by the hair and was holding a dagger to his throat.

Charlie placed a foot on the doorstep. "Sarah, no!"

Arvin halted and jabbed the tip of the double-edged blade into Moran's neck deep enough to draw blood. "Shut up and back off, old man, or so help me, your friend will wind up exactly like Bokor."

Fargo was tempted to resort to his Colt. Moran was a wreck; his nose had been crushed, his lips pulped, and half his front teeth were either shattered or missing. In addition, one eye was discolored and swelling, and there were welts all over his face. The Dirt Breathers had beaten him within an inch of his life.

Vrittan did as Sarah had instructed, and she brought Moran past the doorway. The dagger never wavered. "I want the stallion," she gruffly announced.

"You can't have him," Fargo said.

"Oh?" Sarah dug the knife in deeper. Moran winced and whimpered, too weak and dazed to resist. "This pig is a goner unless you agree. Your horse for his life."

Charlie glanced at Fargo in silent appeal. They were

both aware it was no bluff. Just as they were both aware that without the pinto, their prospects of reaching civilization were slim. Fargo tried to think of a way to stall. "I'll agree to the trade on one condition. Moran and Olivia must both be handed over."

Sarah bared her teeth like a wolverine about to bite. "You're in no position to make demands. It's Moran for the horse. Take it or leave it."

"What about Olivia?" This from Charlie.

"Forget her!" Sarah was practically beside herself. "Are you hard of hearing as well as stunted? Have the stallion brought over right this minute or Moran goes to meet his Maker." To stress her point, she flicked the dagger across the Air Breather's jaw, cutting deep into his flesh.

Crimson spurted, and Moran automatically reached up, only to have his palm slashed from his little finger to his thumb.

"I told you not to move!" Sarah raged. "So much as twitch a muscle and I'll slit your throat anyway!" She shook the dagger at Fargo. "See this blood? It's on your shoulders. His life will be, too, if you don't get a damn move on!"

"Simmer down. We'll go fetch him," Fargo said. Nudging Vrittan, he backed away and waited until they were out of earshot to say, "There's no way in hell I'm turning my horse over to her. We need an idea and we need it now."

"I'm open to any suggestions."

"I'll ride the stallion to the cabin and tell her I won't hand him over until she lets go of your friend. The moment she does, have one of your people pick her off."

"What about the rest of the Dirt Breathers? They won't take kindly to Arvin being shot. They'll kill Moran before he can take two steps, and will be hankering to do the same to you."

"I'll get Moran out of there," Fargo promised, hoping he sounded more confident than he felt. They had to cover a lot of open space to reach the woods.

Charlie sighed and commented, "I wish there were another way. I told you before I don't believe in killing for killing's sake."

"Then do it for the sake of all those who will die if Arvin isn't stopped."

"You're forgetting Olivia. The Dirt Breathers will kill her out of spite if we harm a hair on Sarah's insane head."

Fargo was tired of bickering. Vrittan was a well-meaning coot but indecisive as hell. Yes, risks were involved, but something had to be done. Since Vrittan didn't have the stomach for it, the course of action was up to him. "Would you rather take Arvin alive?"

Nodding enthusiastically, Charlie answered, "If it's at all possible, yes, by all means. With her our prisoner, the Dirt Breathers will do whatever we demand."

"Can you handle her by your lonesome while I keep the Dirt Breathers busy?" Fargo needed to know.

"Try me and find out."

"Tell the others to be ready to rush the cabin," Fargo directed. "I'll get my horse." He deemed it best not to tell the prospector that what he had in mind might get some of them killed. The time had come to end the feud once and for all, with or without Vrittan's cooperation.

Before stepping into the stirrups, Fargo shoved the Henry into the saddle scabbard. For close-in work the Colt was best. He kneed the Ovaro into a slow walk, taking his sweet time just to annoy Arvin. The angrier she was, the less the chance she might suspect he was up to something.

Charlie was waiting at the tree line. "We're all set. At my signal the others will come to our aid."

Fargo rode on by. "Stay behind me and be ready." Switching the reins to his left hand, he rested his right on his hip. Arvin was watching them like a hawk watching prey, her dagger gouging into the side of Moran's neck. The rifle still poked from the window, the revolver from the doorway.

"Hurry it up, damn it!" Sarah shouted.

Fargo saw her whisper over her shoulder to whoever

held the revolver. They were as transparent as glass. Arvin had no intention of honoring her end of the swap. Once he reined up, the Dirt Breathers inside would blast him from the saddle and riddle Charlie and Moran, leaving Sarah free to do as she pleased with the Ovaro.

Smiling and giving a little wave as if he were the world's biggest idiot, Fargo casually lowered his hand closer to his Colt. When he reached the cabin he would need a distraction, something to gain him two or three seconds before the Dirt Breathers cut loose. And he had just the thing.

"You can let Moran go now!" Charlie yelled when they were still ten yards out.

"Not until I'm holding the pinto's reins," Sarah countered. She was showing more teeth than a politician who has just been reelected. As well she should, given that she believed she had them right where she wanted them.

Fargo gauged the narrowing distance carefully. He had to put his plan into effect at just the right instant. Continuing to playact, he said, "After you have my horse, maybe you'll be willing to talk about releasing Olivia."

"Maybe," Sarah said, her grin growing.

The muzzle of the rifle in the window rose a hair.

"Looks like this is good-bye, big fella," Fargo said, bending as if to pat the Ovaro's neck. Suddenly hauling on the reins, he jabbed his spurs against its rear legs. The stallion did as he had been trained it to do, and reared. Now neither the man in the window nor the one on the doorway had a clear shot at him. Another jab of his spurs sent the pinto prancing forward.

"Don't shoot!" Sarah Arvin shrieked at her assassins. "You might hit the horse!"

Kicking his boots free of the stirrups, Fargo gripped the saddle horn and shifted his weight. The stallion started to drop onto all fours, and as it did, he reined sharply to the right, causing it to swing into Arvin and Moran. Both were bowled over. At the selfsame instant, he drew the Colt and pushed clear.

The man behind the curtains parted them to see better. In midair Fargo triggered two shots into the Dirt

Breather's chest. Landing on his boot heels, he whirled just as the other gunman burst outside. The man raised his Smith and Wesson but Fargo triggered a shot faster. Wrenching free of the other's grasp as the Dirt Breather toppled, he hurtled indoors, a revolver in each hand.

Pale figures filled the cabin. Fargo blasted an onrushing apparition in the face. He downed a knife-wielding attacker on his left, shot a woman brandishing an axe on his right. More Dirt Breathers swarmed toward him and he fired as fast as his fingers could work the Colt, five, six, seven shots in supremely swift succession. At each shot a Dirt Breather fell. Within heartbeats the floor was littered with convulsing specters.

Others were streaming into the root cellar.

"Olivia?" Fargo bellowed. He aimed at a Dirt Breather about to descend the ladder, but the Smith and Wesson clicked on an empty cylinder. The Colt was also empty. He needed to reload before the Dirt Breathers realized it.

From outside came yells and the drum of boots and shoes. Into the cabin flew several Air Breathers, two men and a woman. In their haste they nearly tripped over some of the bodies. One gaped in astonishment and exclaimed, "My God!"

The last of the Dirt Breathers was poised at the edge of the cellar, about to jump. Each Air Breather fired and each missed. In the blink of an eye the Dirt Breather was gone.

Dropping the Smith and Wesson, Fargo reloaded the Colt. As soon as he slid the last cartridge into the cylinder, he ran to join the three Air Breathers at the root cellar. They were arguing over whether they should follow their enemies into the tunnel.

One gripped the top of the ladder to start down, but Fargo put a hand on the man's arm. "What if they're waiting for us just out of sight?"

Pulling back, the Air Breather licked his lips. "I suppose it would be best to wait until we can do it together."

"Wait here and make sure they don't try anything," Fargo directed. "I'll go see how Charlie is doing."

Vrittan and Moran had taken Sarah Arvin prisoner. Vrittan had a gun on her. Moran had her own dagger pressed against her neck. The prospector's face was bleeding from where she had raked him with her nails, and Moran was leaking blood from the cuts in his neck though he seemed not to care.

"I take it we prevailed?" Charlie said with a smile.

"A lot of them made it underground," Fargo reported. "To end this, we have to go down after them."

Sarah started to cackle but stopped when Moran shifted the point of the dagger to under her chin. She was splotched with dust, her hair disheveled, but otherwise none the worse for wear. "I hope to hell you do go into the mine! Not one of you bastards will make it out alive!"

"She has a point," Charlie conceded. "The Dirt Breathers will have an advantage. They know every branch, every fork. They can lead us in circles while picking us off as they see fit."

"Aren't you forgetting something?" Fargo said. "Olivia wasn't in the cabin. They must have taken her underground with them. We have to go after her."

"Not necessarily," Charlie said, and nodded at Arvin. "The Dirt Breathers will do whatever we demand now that we have their leader. We'll order them to bring Olivia up."

"It won't be that simple, runt," Sarah sneered. "They'll only take orders from me and I'm not about to have them do any such thing."

"You'll do as we tell you," Charlie insisted.

"Or what? You'll have me shot?" Sarah tittered. "Honestly, you old fool. Everyone knows how tenderhearted you are. You couldn't kill me if your life depended on it."

Moran wagged the dagger before her face. "But I could! I can cut you from ear to ear and not bat an eye, bitch."

Sarah gave him a look of utter disdain. "Sure you could. But Charlie isn't about to give the order, and you won't so much as spit without his say-so."

Fargo slid the Colt into its holster. Here they were, bickering again, wasting valuable time. "I'll lead a rescue party underground myself. Send to town for more of your people."

"Very well, but be advised I can't command them to go with you," Charlie said. "It's not my decision to make. It's theirs. We'll hold a meeting and take a vote to find out how many are willing to join you."

That would take hours. Not bothering to hide his frustration, Fargo walked across the clearing to where the Ovaro was cropping grass. First he would picket the pinto, then he was going after Dixon if he had to do it alone. About to reach for the reins, he spied a hulking figure crouched among the trees. "Step out where I can see you!" he hollered, yanking the Henry from the saddle scabbard.

Clarence shuffled into the open, one arm over his eyes to shield them from the sun's harsh glare. Squinting toward the cabin, he whined like a puppy.

Fargo scanned the woods but saw no trace of the other Dirt Breathers from the grotto. Maybe they were waiting for nightfall to return. Or maybe the gunfire had scared them off.

Clarence whined again, and motioned.

"You want to go to your mother, is that it?" Fargo asked, and the giant nodded. "I don't see why not. Walk in front of me. And keep your hands where I can see them at all times."

Happily bobbing his great misshapen head, Clarence extended both arms and hustled past. For all his immense size and strength, he had the mind and heart of a child. Of all the Dirt Breathers, he was the only one Fargo felt any sympathy for.

Charlie and Moran had their backs to the woods, and didn't realize Clarence was there until he was almost on top of them. Startled, they glanced around. Shock and fear rooted them for a second, then Moran raised the dagger for a lethal thrust.

"No!" Fargo barked. "He's not here to harm anyone."

"But it's *him*!" Moran bleated. "The monster! The worst of the lot! He's killed more of us than all the rest combined."

"At her bidding," Fargo said, indicating Arvin.

"What difference in hell does that make?"

Clarence gazed lovingly at Sarah, his huge body stooped over like that of a dog currying its master's favor. He whined some more, and tentatively held out an enormous hand.

Arvin was as stunned as the others had been, but not for the same reason. "You dare come back here?" she demanded, slapping Clarence's fingers away. "You dare show your misbegotten face after letting me down?"

Pressing the hand to his massive chest, Clarence whimpered.

"I gave you a simple job!" Sarah railed. "All you had to do was guard the stallion and keep it hidden! But you botched it! And now you come walking in here to beg my forgiveness when you should be trying to help me. Have you no brains whatsoever?"

Clarence withered under her verbal onslaught, his immense size and strength rendered impotent by the one thing he was powerless to resist. His own love.

"It's moments like these that make me wonder why I didn't drown you the day you were born," Sarah plunged her verbal knife deeper. "Until you came along I lived a perfectly ordinary life. But ever since then it's been a living hell. Perhaps your father had the right idea. Perhaps I'm better off without you."

"It's not his fault," Fargo said.

Sarah rounded on him in fury. "What the hell do you know? You didn't bring this abomination into the world. You didn't abide his never-ending bumbling and bungling." Straightening, she bestowed an imperious stare on her offspring. "Here's your chance to make good,

Clarence. Prove my trust in you isn't misplaced. Kill these three fools."

"What?" Charlie Vrittan said in alarm.

"The devil you say!" Moran exclaimed.

Fargo sidled to the left. "Don't listen to her, Clarence."

Sarah ignored them. "What are you waiting for, son? If you truly care for me as much as you would like me to believe, then prove it. Take care of these bastards so we can be on our way."

Clarence groaned, as if in pain, his huge hands rising to either side of his face. For a few moments he was a virtual statue. Then he dropped his arms to his sides, let out a bestial roar, and attacked.

12

"Clarence, don't!" Skye Fargo shouted, but his plea fell on deaf ears. The giant ripped into Charlie Vrittan and Moran before they could defend themselves. A backward swipe of a gigantic arm catapulted Charlie head over heels even as Clarence's other hand closed on Moran's windpipe, and constricted. Fargo went to shoot but Clarence swivelled, and it was Moran, struggling and squawking, who filled the Henry's sights. Skipping to the left for a clear shot, Fargo didn't see the hide-covered foot sweeping toward his midsection until it slammed into his ribs with the impact of a runaway steam engine. It felt as if his entire chest had caved in.

The next Fargo knew, he was on his back in the dust, his ribs on fire. In front of him, Clarence was throttling the life from Moran. Charlie lay where he had fallen, either unconscious or dead.

Out of the cabin barreled the three Air Breathers Fargo had left to watch the root cellar. They had heard the racket, and as they came through the doorway they leaped to help Moran. Since they couldn't fire at such close quarters, they beat Clarence about the head and shoulders with their guns. But they might as well have been beating on a boulder for all the effect they had.

Fargo placed his hands under him to rise, and was promptly slammed flat as someone crashed down on top of him. Thinking one of the Air Breathers had tripped over him, he gripped a dangling arm to push the man off. Suddenly a face flopped in front of his. It was Moran, his neck a mangled ruin, his eyes wide in the disbelief he experienced at the moment he died. Shoving the body, Fargo heaved upright. He spotted the Henry and scooped it up as the clearing rocked to the boom of a gunshot.

Clarence had an Air Breather in each hand and was doing to them as he had done to Moran: strangling them alive. The two men kicked and bucked, but they were kittens in the iron grasp of a tiger.

The third Air Breather, the woman, was the one who had fired. Holding her revolver in both hands, she took precise aim at the giant's head. "Drop them!" she hollered.

Clarence did no such thing. Pivoting, he hurled one of the men at her. The woman tried to skip aside but she was much too slow and was bowled over, allowing Clarence to wrap his other hand around the head of the Air Breather still in his grasp, and begin at twist.

Fargo sighted along the Henry. He felt sorry for the stripling, but he would be damned if he would stand there and let another life be extinguished. At a range of less than eight feet he fired directly into Clarence's torso. The impact of the heavy-caliber slug was enough to flatten most men in their tracks, but all the giant youth did was blink.

The man in the grip of Clarence's giant hands was Fred, the Air Breather who had been wounded earlier. Now he screamed, a cry torn from the depths of his being even as his head was torn from his shoulders. A rending of flesh, a loud crack, and the deed was done.

Fargo worked the Henry's lever to eject the spent cartridge and feed a new one into the chamber. He glanced down for just a heartbeat, and something crashed against his temple, staggering him. The world spun, and he heard the woman shriek. As his vision cleared, he saw Fred's head upside down next to his left boot. Clarence had thrown it at him.

The giant now had hold of the woman and was raising her high into the air, apparently a prelude to dashing her brains out on the ground.

Fargo fired, worked the lever, and fired again.

Jarred backward, Clarence regained his balance, uttered a roar that shook the mountains, and flung the woman to the earth. The crunch and crackle of breaking bones testified to the raw brute power of his granite physique.

Molding his cheek to the Henry's stock, Fargo fixed a bead on Clarence's forehead as the youth turned toward him. He touched his finger to the trigger, and hesitated.

Tears were streaming from Clarence's eyes, a torrent that had dampened his cheeks and chin. He wore a pleading expression, his need mirrored in his gaze, as he coiled to spring.

"Damn your mother to hell," Fargo growled, and stroked the trigger. For all of ten seconds after the immense frame toppled, he stood with his head bowed. Then someone moaned, and he stirred and looked around.

Charlie Vrittan was sitting up. He had a knot above his right eye, but he was fortunate compared to the rest. Surveying the carnage, he recoiled at the sight of the severed head. "God Almighty!"

Fargo bent over the Air Breather Clarence had tossed at the woman. The man's neck was broken. He checked the rest, but it was futile.

"The boy killed every last one?" Charlie exclaimed, rising. Aghast, he stumbled from one body to the next as if drunk. "Even poor Martha. She and Olivia were very close."

The mention of Dixon reminded Fargo of the woman who hated her and wanted her dead. "Where's Sarah?" he asked, rotating three hundred and sixty degrees. In all the confusion she had disappeared. He glanced at Charlie, and the same answer occurred to them both. As one, they sped inside and over to the root cellar.

"We're too late," the old prospector said.

Olivia Dixon was as good as dead, and Fargo blamed himself. He should have kept an eye on Arvin. She had played them all for lunkheads, siccing her son on them to keep them occupied while she made her escape. Coldhearted and devious didn't begin to describe her.

"We should head to town for help," Charlie proposed. "On horseback we can be there and return in an hour, maybe less."

"We'll be too late," Fargo said. He was sure Olivia would be dead by then. "The two of us must do it alone."

"Are you loco? There are still plenty of Dirt Breathers left. And Sarah will be expecting us. She'll have a suitable welcome prepared."

"Not if we don't give her time to set one up." Fargo stepped to the ladder and lowered his right boot onto the second rung.

"It's the same as holding a loaded gun to our own heads," Charlie objected. "I refuse to commit suicide."

Fargo's estimation of Vrittan dropped a little. "Would Olivia refuse if Sarah was holding you captive? Did those followers of yours who just died for your cause hold back when Clarence went berserk?'

Charlie bent to study the tunnel entrance. "You just don't savvy, do you? I haven't set foot down there since Sarah and her brood drove me out. And I never was all that comfortable being underground to begin with."

"A prospector who is afraid of mines?" Fargo asked skeptically.

"Prospector, hell." Charlie squatted, removed his floppy hat, and ran his stubby fingers through his gray hair. "This was the first time in my life I ever went looking for gold. Beginners luck, you might say." He shoved his hat back on. "I was like everyone else. All fired up because of the big strike in California. So I quit my job and headed West."

"What kind of job?" Fargo asked merely to put Vrittan more at ease. The man was going along whether he wanted to or not, but he would like Vrittan to think it was his idea.

"I was a performer with the Hailey and Armbrewster Traveling Circus, out of New York City. Part of a troupe of seven dwarves. Tumblers and acrobats and the like." Charlie wistfully smiled. "I miss those days. If I get out of this mess alive, I'm going to look Mr. Armbrewster up and beg for my old job back."

"Do you suppose Olivia Dixon wants to get out of this alive?"

Charlie frowned. "You fight dirty, Mr. Fargo," he said petulantly.

"Dixon is a fine woman. She sided with you of her own free will, and paid for it with the loss of her brother. Can you turn your back on her now, when she needs help the most?"

Smacking the floor in irritation, Charlie grumbled, "You missed your calling, friend. You should have been a lawyer. You'd never lose a case." He slowly rose and moved to the ladder. "I have an idea where the Dirt Breathers took her. It'll take about fifteen minutes to get there so we'd best light a shuck."

The tunnel entrance was mired in darkness. Fargo descended a few rungs and stopped. He wouldn't put it past Sarah to have some of her followers hidden just out of sight with orders to rush anyone who climbed down into the cellar. Shifting sideways, he pushed off and jumped. As he landed he leveled the Henry, but no pale forms came storming out to slay him.

"Is it safe?" Charlie nervously asked.

"For now. Hurry up."

Vrittan gripped each side rail. But instead of taking the rungs one at a time, he placed his left foot against the left rail and his right foot against the right one and slid all the way down as slick as could be. "A trick I learned with the circus," he explained, grinning.

Fargo moved to the tunnel. He heard nothing, saw nothing. "Lead the way. But be careful we don't become separated."

"Shouldn't we take a lantern?" Charlie inquired, pointing at one on a shelf.

Fargo had been debating that very question. The Dirt Breathers would see a light from a long way off and be drawn to it like moths to a flame. By the same token, without it, they might blunder into a pit or some other nasty surprise. And it was worth bearing in mind the Dirt Breathers couldn't tolerate bright light. He decided to compromise. "We'll take it, but we won't use it unless we have to."

"Lordy, I hope you know what you're doing."

Fargo made sure the tank was full before setting out. The quiet was unnerving, more so the further they traveled. At the first junction Fargo halted to listen and heard only his companion's anxious breathing. The man was scared. He hoped Vrittan wouldn't bolt when they encountered the Dirt Breathers.

"The sooner we get this over with, the happier I'll be," Charlie whispered, taking the right branch.

"I've been through this section," Fargo mentioned to allay some of his fear. "There aren't any booby traps."

"Only because none of us knew about it."

For minutes that seemed like hours they wound steadily deeper into the belly of the earth. Fargo was glad he had the old man to guide him, because without Vrittan, he would be hopelessly lost. Twice they heard distant voices that faded. Once they heard the clang of metal on metal. Fargo thought it might be a signal, but nothing ever happened and it wasn't repeated. He had lost count of the junctions they passed when they came to one more, and Charlie stopped.

"We're close now. We have to be on our guard."

"Close to what?" Fargo asked.

"The largest chamber in the mine. A cavern where I found a stockpile of old tools and timbers the Spaniards left behind. The gold ore was at a lot lower depth. Of course, I have no idea where Sarah moved it."

They hadn't gone ten feet when Fargo heard the murmur of voices.

"I was right!" Charlie whispered. "Maybe now is a good time to light that lantern."

"Not yet."

The murmur became a drone, tongueless men and women's garbled speech, over a dozen conversations taking place simultaneously. Ahead, on the right, the tunnel wall seemed to fold in on itself. It was actually an opening wide enough for a stagecoach to roll through. Peering beyond, Fargo beheld the natural cavern Vrittan spoke of. Fifty yards long and half as wide, the walls rose to a vaulted apex lost in indigo heights. Along the far wall was old mining equipment and a row of stacked crates.

Of more interest to Fargo were the twenty or so Dirt Breathers gathered in the center. To the left sat a long table, and on it lay a woman, evidently bound. Fargo couldn't see her face but he didn't have to. They had round Olivia Dixon.

From somewhere on the right came several more Dirt Breathers, led by none other than Sarah Arvin. Her blonde hair was unmistakable. She was carrying something Fargo couldn't quite make out. "Friends! Dear ones!" she cried, flinging her arms into the air. "May I have your attention!"

The muttering stopped. Arvin strolled through their midst to the table, and turned. Her teeth flashed white. "We lost many of our brothers and sisters this day, but we have not lost the war! Far from it! For thanks to my son, who gave his life in defense of our cause, the enemy we most despise has been slain! I saw Charlie Vrittan die with my own eyes!"

Whoops and bellows greeted the news.

"She thinks I'm dead?" Charlie whispered, and snickered.

"Quiet." Fargo was concerned about late arrivals who might show up and catch them lurking in the tunnel.

"The Air Breathers are leaderless!" Sarah crowed. "They will be disorganized, confused. At long last we have an opportunity to finish them off. Tonight, while they cower in their wretched buildings, we will burn their town down around their miserable ears. Those who live will take to the hills where we can track them down and dispose of them at our leisure."

More whoops and yells rose to the ceiling.

"After all these years, after all the hardship and tears, our day has come! Once our enemies are disposed of, the gold will finally and truly be ours!" Sarah held aloft the object she had been carrying. "In this satchel is some of the ore we have cached. The ore that will make all of us rich. I brought it here because I like the sweet irony of using it to dispose of yet another enemy. Someone who was once a dear friend, but who made the mistake of siding with Vrittan against us. Against those who only had her best interests at heart."

Sarah set the satchel onto the table next to Olivia.

The Dirt Breathers looked from the bag of gold to their leader, confusion painted across their faces.

Sarah smiled wickedly, "Haven't you ever smashed a pumpkin to a pulp?"

Charlie nudged Fargo. "She'll do it, too."

"Come on," Fargo whispered, and crept into the cavern. Staying low and close to the right-hand wall, he glided toward the table.

Sarah was fiddling with the satchel. There was a loud *thunk,* and she raised something over her head. "Do you see this chunk of ore? It must weigh ten pounds. And it has such a nice jagged edge. Think of what it will do to our captive's pretty head when I bring it crashing down on her skull!"

Olivia rose onto her elbows. "Do it and get it over with, damn you!"

"And deprive myself of the pleasure of savoring your fear?" Sarah gloated. "I've waited too long for this. Next to Charlie, you're the one I despise most. Now your treachery will be repaid in full."

"You were the one who turned against us, remember? The treachery is yours, not mine. And don't brand me a coward when I'm not. I've never been afraid of you, and I'm not afraid now. If my time has come, so be it."

"You talk big, but let's see how brave you are after I break a few of your fingers."

"My fingers? But you just said—"

"You didn't honestly expect me to kill you outright, did you?" Sarah rejoined. "Hell, no. I want you to suffer. I want you to feel pain such as you have never known. I won't split your head until the very last." Sarah nodded at two men. One seized Dixon and held her down while the other untied the rope around her wrists, then stretched her arms as far as they would reach.

Olivia struggled, but the men were too strong.

Intent on the imminent torture, the Dirt Breathers pressed closer.

As yet no one had noticed Fargo and Charlie. Another thirty feet and they were close enough. Handing the lantern to the midget, Fargo whispered, "When I say the word, light it."

Charlie nodded, but it was plain he was more scared than ever and would rather be anywhere other than where they were.

Fargo took another couple of steps and centered the Henry on Sarah Arvin's abundant bosom. He would dearly love to shoot her right then but she was to be his unwitting ace in the hole. "Now!" he whispered.

A match flared, and a moment later a yellow glow radiated outward. The light caught Sarah in the act of raising the glistening piece of ore, and froze her in place. The pallid men holding Dixon recoiled, one throwing a hand over his eyes, while the rest of the Dirt Breathers were momentarily transfixed in astonishment.

Fargo took several steps so everyone could clearly see the Henry. "No one is to move or Arvin takes the first bullet!"

A few Dirt Breathers took impulsive steps toward him but were grabbed by others. Sarah, herself, didn't seem the least little surprised, and smiled mockingly.

"Well, well. So my useless son didn't kill you as I had hoped. And here you are, come to rescue the damsel in distress."

"Put down the ore," Fargo commanded. He hoped Arvin would have sense enough to comply, but he should have known better.

"Go ahead! Pull the trigger! As soon as you do, you're a dead man." Sarah swept the assembled snowy specters with a wave of her hand. "Rush him! Tear the bastard limb from limb. Him and the runt, both!"

The Dirt Breathers looked at one another.

"You heard me!" Sarah shouted, and pointed to Fargo. "Ever since this man arrived he has been a thorn in our side. If we let him live, he'll report us to the army and a detachment will be sent to take us into custody and confiscate our gold!" She paused so it would sink in. "That's right! They will take our ore. All our hard work, all the friends and family we've lost, all the years of heartache and misery, will have been for nothing."

Fargo could see her impassioned plea was having an impact. Vrittan had it all wrong; she was the one who should have been a lawyer. The crazed looks that came over the Dirt Breathers made him think Vrittan had been right about one thing. Breathing that gas in the lower levels of the mine had done something to their minds. Maybe the gas was why the Spaniards stopped mining to begin with.

"What are you waiting for?" Sarah urged her followers on. "He can't shoot all of you. After him! Now!"

"But I can drop you!" Fargo declared. "And with you gone, who will lead them? Who will speak for them now that they can't speak for themselves? You're the one person they can't do without."

Some of the Dirt Breathers nodded. They were half-crazed but they weren't too far gone to recognize the truth when they heard it.

Fargo didn't dare allow Arvin more time to persuade them. "You two!" he shouted at the men beside the table. "Help Olivia Dixon down, then join the rest."

"Don't listen to him!" Sarah screeched, and launched into a string of obscenities when the men did as Fargo instructed.

Fargo expected Olivia to rush to his side. But the moment her feet touched the cavern floor, she sprang at Sarah, grabbed handfuls of lustrous golden hair, and roughly dragged the taller woman around to the end of the table. Sarah was bent backwards, nearly in half, and couldn't punch or kick to free herself.

"I brought you a present!" Olivia declared, shoving Arvin against the wall.

Caterwauling like a catamount, Sarah whisked the

piece of ore over her head and threw herself at Dixon. Had the blow landed, there was no doubt Olivia's head would have split wide open.

Fargo got there first. He blocked the ore with his rifle barrel, then buried the stock in Sarah's stomach. As she folded, sucking air and sputtering, he tore the ore from her grasp and thrust it at Olivia. "Hold onto this. If she gives you any trouble, use it."

"Look out!" Charlie cried.

Several Dirt Breathers were rushing them. Fargo dropped one with a snap shot from the hip, dropped a second with a slug to the chest. For a few seconds his eyes were off Sarah and she seized the chance to scramble across the floor toward her followers.

"Kill them! Kill them all!"

Olivia started to go after the madwoman, but Fargo snagged her arm and pushed her at Vrittan. "Run for your lives!" Olivia balked, forcing Charlie to clamp hold of her wrist and haul her after him as a howling pack of Dirt Breathers swooped across the cavern.

Fargo had used two of the fifteen rounds in the Henry's tubular magazine. He fired a third as he backpedaled, and a pale bundle of muscle and bones pitched to earth. Then there was no time to count the shots. Pumping the lever, he fired again and again and again. Each slug dropped a Dirt Breather but there was always another to take their place. He cored a wild-eyed beanstalk through the forehead and drilled a frenzied banshee through the heart. He sent a round into one old enough to be his grandfather and another into one younger than Clarence. And still they came, spreading out to try and outflank him. He downed two on the right and another on the left, blunting the attempt.

Fargo reached the tunnel. Charlie and Olivia were a little farther on, waiting for him to catch up. He sprinted to them, snatched the lantern, and set it down in the center of the passage.

"What the dickens are you doing?" Charlie asked, perplexed.

"No time to explain," Fargo said, pushing them. "Run!

Run like hell!" He ran, too, never once taking his eyes off the cavern entrance, and when he saw the remaining Dirt Breathers stream into the tunnel, howling at the top of their lungs, he halted and sank to one knee.

Sarah Arvin was in the lead. Screeching the loudest of the lot and wielding a long-bladed knife, she flew down the tunnel. The lantern meant nothing to her. She was the one Dirt Breather at home above and below ground. But those behind her slowed, unable to bear the bright gleam.

"Fargo! Come on!" Charlie bawled.

"Keep going!" Fargo responded, and set the Henry's front bead on the base of the lantern. Aligning the rear sight with the front, he filled his lungs and held his breath. Arvin was thirty feet from the lantern. Then twenty. Then ten. Fargo waited until she was almost on top of it, and smoothly stroked the trigger.

The lantern exploded, spewing a roiling fireball that filled the tunnel from side to side, and a crackling sheet of flame enveloped Sarah. Her dress combusted, turning her into a moving bonfire. Shrieking horribly, she ran a few more yards, then stopped and swatted vainly at the flames. They were spreading too rapidly. Uttering a strangled snarl of baffled rage, she lurched toward Fargo, her hands hooked into claws, her lips drawn back from her perfect teeth.

"For God's sake, shoot her!" Olivia implored.

The Dirt Breathers were retreating into the cavern. Only Arvin was left, her entire body aflame, yet still she staggered determinedly toward them, driven by her insane yet indomitable will.

"Shoot her!" Olivia cried.

Fargo took aim, closed his eyes, and fired.

No one had anything to say until after they were in the clearing outside the cabin with the sun warm on their backs and birds chirping merrily in the trees.

Charlie removed his hat and said gratefully, "It's over at last. Once you notify the Army, the Dirt Breathers are finished for good."

Fargo noticed the ore Olivia still held. "May I?" he

said, and examined the brass-yellow cubes and nodules. He wasn't a prospector but he knew a little about gold. "Is the rest of the ore like this piece?"

"Sure is," Charlie said proudly. "How much do you reckon a ton or two of it will be worth?"

"Not very much."

Charlie laughed, thinking it was a joke, then sobered when he saw Fargo was serious. "How can you say a thing like that?"

"All those deaths, all those families whose lives were ruined." Fargo dropped the ore in the dust. "And all for a bunch of damned pyrite."

"Py-what?"

"Fool's gold, Charlie. The vein you found was nothing but fool's gold." Fargo hooked an arm around Olivia and headed for the Ovaro. He wanted some time alone with her, wanted to feel her soft body pressed against his. In a day or two he would head out. But until then, there was nothing like a warm and willing woman to help a man forget.

LOOKING FORWARD!

**The following is the opening
section from the next novel in the exciting
Trailsman series from Signet:**

THE TRAILSMAN #252
Kansas City Swindle

*Kansas City, 1859
Thievery may be a sin, but for the most beautiful
of thieves it won't be the first . . .*

Nimble Svenson scuttled down through the Kansas City train yard between the side-railed cars until he found the right one. Looking from side to side, he swung up onto its platform and rapped on the fancy, cut- and etched-glass panel in the door.

After he'd rapped three times, the brass knob turned and the door opened.

"Yes?" said the man in the shadows. He was big, nearly as big around as he was tall, and a fat cigar jutted from his mouth. He wore a black back-east suit and a silk vest the color of emeralds, and his voice was as deep and sonorous as a death knell.

Nimble swept the hat off his head. "Howdy, M-Mr. Stacy," Nimble said with smile that was just for show. Stacy made him awfully nervous, if for no other reason than that he was alive. "Mr. Stacy, I think I got the answer to all your problems."

Stacy stared at him for a few seconds, seemed to study on him, which made Nimble all the more anxious. But then Stacy stepped back and opened the door wide. "Come in," he said.

"Sure, yessir, Mr. Stacy," Nimble muttered, and scuttled down the car's narrow hallway in the big man's wake.

Stacy had to duck down just a little, Nimble noticed, and his sides brushed both walls of the little hall. *He'd have a hard pocket to pick,* Nimble thought automatically, and then he brushed the idea from his mind. No more picking pockets, no more badger games, no more trying to find a partner that wouldn't run out on him and take the cash, at least not for a while. This was going to be the night the hit the big score.

Unconsciously, he straightened and walked a little taller. Rich. By God, he was going to be a rich man.

Or at least, he'd have some coin in his pocket for a change.

Light hit Nimble in the face as Mr. Stacy suddenly emerged into the parlor of the car, leaving Nimble blinking before the lamps, his hat in his hand.

"Tell him," Stacy said, and hiked his thumb toward a new man, one Nimble hadn't met before, who was seated across the little room, a folded newspaper in his lap. From what Nimble could see, the printing sure didn't look like English. A cigar burned in the cut glass ashtray at his side, although it was longer and thinner than the one clamped in Stacy's teeth.

Nimble looked from the stranger to Stacy and back again.

"It's all right, Mr. Svenson," the man in the chair said. His voice was different from Stacy's, thin and icy, kind of, and his accent was strange. Foreign, cultured. He stood up. He was a good bit taller than Nimble, but not so frighteningly tall as Mr. Stacy. A god bit thinner, too. Almost skeletal. He held out a slender hand, and Nimble took it.

"Nimble, if'n you don't mind," Nimble said, his voice cracking a little in the middle. "Everybody calls me that."

The handshake was exceedingly dry and firm, and a sparkling diamond pinkie ring rubbed briefly against Nimble's hand. It took all of Nimble's self control not to slip it off him.

"Very good. Nimble, then," said the man, smiling slightly. "I am Vladimir Korchenko." He nodded his head in the suggestion of a bow.

"Nice to meetcha, Mr. Korchenko," Nimble said. He was still trying to figure the angle on this. When he'd talked to Stacy before, he'd assumed he was acting alone. Nobody had said anything about some fancy-pants dude from Russia or Hungary or someplace horning in.

Korchenko sat back down and gestured toward the chair opposite his. It was upholstered in red velvet, as was Korchenko's, and looked to be cozy enough and big enough to sleep in. There'd been many a night that Nimble would have paid good money to sleep in a chair like this one.

Nobody had to ask him twice. He sat down. The chair was like a cloud.

"Cigar?" asked Korchenko, and offered a monogrammed, silver case from his inside pocket. "Or perhaps you would prefer one of Mr. Stacy's. I find them too harsh, but to each his own."

"Oh no," replied Nimble, and quickly took a cigar. He ran it under his nose. It was a beauty, soaked in cognac if he wasn't mistaken. He stuck it into his pocket and gave it a pat. "This'll be just dandy, and it's right nice of you. I'll just save it for later on, if'n you don't mind."

Korchenko lifted a brow, but that was all. He closed

the case with a click and replaced it. "Certainly, Nimble, certainly," he said, and leaned back. He picked up his cigar, rolled the ash off against the side of the ashtray, and took a puff. "You have news for us? You have found our man?"

Nimble nodded. "I sure have. Just the right feller, too." He eyed Korchenko's brandy snifter, which he'd just spotted.

"Franklin?" Korchenko said to Stacy. "A glass for our friend."

Franklin Stacy, then. This put a whole new twist on the deal. Korchenko looked to be the boss of Stacy. At least, Nimble was pretty sure of it, since Stacy hadn't perched once since they came in, and now Stacy was at the little bar, pouring out Nimble's drink. And all the time he'd figured that Stacy was the man in charge.

Nimble slouched back and slung his elbow over the arm of the chair. Pretty damned grand, if you asked him. And he had what they needed. The catbird seat, that's what he was in!

Stacy handed him a snifter, and Nimble swirled it under his nose, aping an actor he'd seen in a play one time.

"Real nice, Mr. Korchenko," he said, and he meant it. It was all he could do to keep from chugging down the brandy and asking for more, it was that good. As it was, he took just a sip. It rolled over his tongue and down his throat, smooth as heated honey.

Nimble looked around the car. Cut glass lamps, nice paintings of horses and hounds and such, rich paneling, and lots of gilt, and deep, plush carpets. He remembered the "VK" etched into the glass of the back door, where he'd come in. They didn't rent out Pullman cars this nice, not with a man's own initials cut into it. Korchenko must own it.

"You fellers have got you a real class operation, here," Nimble said with an approving nod. "Yessir, real class."

"Thank you, Nimble," Korchenko said with another

of those bow-nods. "I am so pleased that you approve. And now, who and where is this gentleman whom you have found for us?"

"You boys ever heard of a feller called Skye Fargo?" Nimble asked, swirling his brandy again. He was feeling rather full of himself. And to think he'd had to work up the courage to come looking or Stacy!

Korchenko furrowed his brow and looked at Stacy. Stacy came forward a step and said, "I have, Vladimir." And then he turned to Nimble and arched a brow. "You have found Skye Fargo for us? Here? In Kansas City?"

That "us" sort of bothered Nimble. Shouldn't Stacy have said that he'd found him for Korchenko?

But he said, "Yessir, I sure have. Course, him and me ain't personally acquainted, but I reckon he's just the man you're lookin' for. Couldn't find no better, I'll wager."

Korchenko looked up at Stacy. "You know this man?"

"Only by reputation, Vladimir," Stacy said. "They call him the Trailsman. He is a tall man, I've heard, and conversant in several tongues including those of the natives. He led the Castlerock party through the wilderness, and singlehandedly put an outlaw called Little Tommy Scraggs—and this was a fellow who had murdered seven men—on the gallows."

"Scraggs?" said Korchenko with arched bows and a shake of his head. "These Americans have such colorful names."

"He also whipped the R&G railroad boys," piped up Nimble, who was nearly finished with his brandy. "Caught Sammy Fishback dead to rights, broke up that big strike on the Dead Ringer Mine out in California, and I hear he put the kibosh on some big bank swindle up in Montana, too, and went undercover to do it. Oh, he's a slick one, and he's got guts. Always heard tell that them blue eyes of his could slice right through you, and havin' seem 'em for myself tonight, I'm believin' they're right."

Nimble slid a long glance toward the bar and the decanter. It looked to him like they could afford to give a poor fellow another glass of welcome. "Could I talk you into pourin' me another, Mr. Stacy?" He held out his snifter.

Stacy took it, although he didn't budge in the direction of the bar. "That's correct, Vladimir," he said. To Nimble, he asked, "And he is here? In Kansas City?"

"Yessir, he sure is," Nimble said. He could practically feel the rumble of Stacy's voice through his shoes, even when the man was talking in a conversational tone.

"Right across town at the Purple Garter Saloon," Nimble continued. "I heard him tellin' Miss Rose that he was at loose ends till next month. Reckon you could get him, all right. Reckon you could get him easy. For whatever it is you want him for." He eyed his brandy glass once more, which dangled in Stacy's fingers.

"More brandy for our friend," said Korchenko, and Stacy finally went to the bar.

"Thank you, sir," said a relieved Nimble. That was the best brandy he'd ever had, even better than they'd served at the fancy hotel in Chicago where Eva-Marie Sutcliffe had stolen all his money. The goddamn bitch. "Now, about the payment . . ."

Korchenko held up a finger. "In time, Nimble, in time. Where is this Fargo staying?"

Nimble shrugged. "Right upstairs from the bar, far as I could tell." He grinned suddenly, and rather smarmily. "Sounded like him and Miss Rose was old friends, if'n you know what I mean." He winked at Korchenko knowingly. "You can't miss him. Slim feller. Got him a close-cropped beard and he wears these old bucks."

Korchenko cocked a brow. "Bucks?"

"Buckskin," Stacy explained. "Deerhide. Fringed, like some of the native tribes wear."

"That's right," said Nimble, nodding. "They got fringe on 'em, all right."

"Very god, very good," said Korchenko, at the same

moment that Stacy handed Nimble his second brandy. "I believe you and Mr. Stacy had already agreed on a finder's fee? Five hundred dollars, was it not?"

Just the mention of all that money jarred Nimble—but in a happy way, of course—and he downed the brandy in one gulp. A welcome warmth spread through his belly. "Yessir," he said. "That was . . . uh . . . the figure mentioned."

"Mr. Stacy?" said Korchenko.

Without ceremony, Stacy dropped a small bag of coins into Nimble's lap. He also took his brandy glass.

Nimble opened the bag, but before he could pour the coins out and have a real look at all that money, Korchenko added, "Half now, half if he agrees to do the work."

Nimble peered into the bag. Damn it, Korchenko was right. Only two hundred and fifty.

Nimble pulled the drawstring again. "How'll I know?" he asked, and this time, emboldened by brandy, didn't pretend to smile. "I mean, what's to keep you fellers from skippin' town on me?"

Korchenko stood up. "You have merely my word, Nimble. But I assure you, it is as constant as the Northern star."

Oh, what the hell, thought Nimble. Stacy had put out feelers with several of the fellows in town, and he had happened to come up with somebody good—somebody great—right off the bat, and brought the name to them before anybody else. Hell's bells, he'd come up with the one and only Skye Fargo!

Even if Stacy and Korchenko did skip, at least he was two hundred and fifty bucks richer than he'd been a few minutes ago. And besides, what if Fargo said no to whatever they were planning? He couldn't help that, could he? Of course not!

Besides, he wasn't about to step outside with that fancy-tailored bruiser, Stacy, and fight for the rest of his money, no sir! Stacy could likely bash in his skull with just one finger.

"Okay," Nimble said, and stuck the little pouch in his pocket. "Whatever you say."

"Excellent," said Korchenko, and smiled. His face reminded Nimble of one of those waxwork dummies he'd seen when he was in San Francisco.

"If Mr. Fargo agrees," Korchenko went on, "Mr. Stacy will find you and pay you the balance of your fee. You have no need to worry. Of course, if there is no Mr. Fargo extant, if you have simply brought us a tale with no substance, Mr. Stacy will be collecting the payment he just gave you."

Nimble gulped. He hoped they didn't notice. "Oh, there's a Fargo, all right. Big as life and tough as nails."

Stacy set his brandy snifter on the bar and clasped his hands behind his back. "You will be in the usual place, Mr. Svenson?" he asked flatly.

"The usual place, yeah," said Nimble. His usual place was in the back room of the Addington Bar, where he was currently running a craps game.

Nobody had ever accused Nimble of not knowing when to leave, and seeing as how everybody was up except him, he rose, too.

"Sure, Mr. Korchenko, sure," he said, as affably as he could. That Fargo feller better not skip town anytime soon, or Nimble's ass would be grass. "Nice working with you."

This time he stuck out his hand fist, and Korchenko took it. His hand was as dry and cool as talcum powder. Talcum-powdered wax, Nimble thought, and shuddered.

"Mr. Stacy will find me," he repeated.

No other series has this much historical action!

THE TRAILSMAN

To order call: 1-800-788-6262

Ralph Cotton

**"Gun-smoked, blood-stained, gritty believability...
Ralph Cotton writes the sort of story we all hope
to find within us."**—Terry Johnston

"Authentic Old West detail."—*Wild West Magazine*

JURISDICTION   20547-2
Young Arizona Ranger Sam Burrack has vowed to bring
down a posse of murderous outlaws-and save the impres-
sionable young boy they've befriended.

DEVIL'S DUE   20394-1
The second book in Cotton's "Dead or Alive" series. The
Los Pistoleros gang were the most vicious outlaws
around—but Hart and Roth thought they had them under
control...Until the jailbreak.

Also Available:
BORDER DOGS   19815-8
BLOOD MONEY   20676-2
BLOOD ROCK   20256-2

To order call: 1-800-788-6262